WHIPS AND SPURS AND MURDER

Book Eleven: The Fiona Fleming Cozy Mysteries

PATTI LARSEN

Cover design by Christina Gaudet
www.castlekeepcreations.com

Thanks, Kirstin!

ISBN-13: 978-1-988700-95-3

CHAPTER ONE

There were times when I made truly bad choices in life, moments when I knew better but I just couldn't seem to help myself. You know what I mean, right? How logic and common sense seem to diverge with the powerful urge to act despite the innate understanding such actions will likely get you into a world of trouble and may not, in the end, be worth it? And, despite knowing all that, no matter how much you work to convince yourself some things are better left undone, let go, abandoned, you just can't seem to allow yourself the freedom to be a good, normal person and simply mind your own business.

Wait. Was that just me? Sigh.

Yeah. Just me. Okay then.

Not that I was actively having this particular conversation in my head while I used the low-hanging branch of a nearby maple tree to vault over the chain-link fence. At least, I don't recall if I was berating myself when I landed like a well-practiced sneak thief, my knees flexing when I let them absorb my weight when I hit the ground on the other side, ducking low and scooting down the line of the fence toward the long, narrow building on the other side of the decorative white rails of the paddock. No, I'm pretty sure that my mind was simply intent on not getting caught as I hustled on sneakered feet toward the back of the nearest stable, the sound of voices nearby making my stomach clench though I didn't for a second regret my break and enter.

Nope. Not this girl. I had a wedding to witness, and I'd be damned if anyone was going to keep me from seeing Alicia Conway in her gorgeous white dress.

Okay, so I was imagining she'd be wearing a floofy, puffy, princessesque gown of unimaginable beauty that would put my own wedding selection to shame. Mind you, she was a tiny little blonde thing, perfectly suited to the whole elaborate fantasy that was the modern wedding dream. Me? A bit too tall (according to Sophia Bell at The Bride Boudoir), a bit too wide in the hips (thanks for that one, Robert, because my darling cousin just had to be walking by when I was trying dresses on, didn't he?) and my hair, apparently, was the wrong shade, my complexion just a bit too provincial, to make the perfect, pristine, pinup bride (that was all on me, I admit it).

Not that I cared, though, honestly. I was marrying the man of my dreams. That was all the detail I chose to consider. I got to spend the rest of my days with Crew Turner in my life, in my heart, in bed next to me... so society's ideals of what I should look like on the day I actually tied the knot?

Whatever.

Sure, yeah, I know, I was deluding myself, but it was my delusion, so I got to lie and say it didn't bother me. While obsessing over my (former?) friend's wedding to the point I drove up the mountain on the switchback road to the rear entrance to the Marie Patterson Olympic Equestrian Center, parked behind a bank of bushes, climbed an obliging tree, hopped the fence and now, as surely as I'd lost my marbles, was creeping like a hunted fugitive or assassin-for-hire through the compound toward the main building where I could only imagine the amazingness that was a Patterson wedding— Alicia's incredible talent for detail and design aside— would presently be unfolding.

And there was no way in hell Fiona Fleming was going to miss it.

No, I wasn't above B&E. Despite the loose promise I made to the man I loved before he left town to return to California for an undisclosed reason I hadn't pressed him about, despite my father's pleas with me to just keep my distance and my own internal arguments assuring myself the last place in the world I needed to be today, at this moment, was here, skulking like a criminal, like an unwelcome guest, just for a chance to see my friends get married.

If Crew wondered why I didn't push him for information when the mysterious phone call he'd received carried him away from me for a few days, he didn't put it together with Alicia and Jared's wedding. Or, if he had, he didn't say so out loud.

"You weren't invited," he said, sadly at least, kindly if blunt about it while I watched him unload his carry-on from the back seat of my car, his face creased in worry, the airport doors swishing open to beckon him inside. "Fee, just let it go. Please."

Um-hum.

He was right about that. I let one hand glide over the trim under the wide, low window that served as a lookout for the horse stall I passed, the siding slippery under my fingers, lingering odor of equine occupation making my nose twitch. The whole freaking town had been invited, hadn't they? Even Rosebert. Snarl. I think maybe if Daisy's half-sister hadn't rubbed that particular tidbit in my face yesterday, perhaps logic and practicality might have won the battle.

Except she did, didn't she? Right there in the entry to Sammy's Coffee, flashing the invitation in my face like some prized possession, the efforts of a childish mind to trigger my anger, to make me do something stupid, to raise the wrath of my redheaded stubbornness.

Well, it worked. I exhaled softly as I peeked

around the corner of the barn, the sound of hooves clip-clopping by. I watched the tail-end (literally) of a large bay gelding stroll past, a small woman in a golf shirt and breeches, boots to her knees and a helmet on her head at his side. He towered over her, snorting softly against her forearm before they disappeared through the wide-open entry to the stable. With them vanished into the dim interior, the central yard stood empty, the five matching buildings facing the elaborate and ostentatious (judging the décor, who, me?) fountain splashing heartily in the middle of the ridiculously big and parklike space.

My jaw clenched while I shoved down my furious reaction to Rose's successful tweak of my temper. Thing was, I knew I hadn't been the only one in Reading to be left off the guest list. I inhaled before hurrying across the center of the stable area, head high, pretending I was supposed to be there, while my mind churned. Sure, there were other exceptions, and they hardly surprised me. Like Dad. Mom. Daisy. Crew. Despite the fact I got it, I understood with precise reasoning exactly why I was on that list (or, at least, that the Pattersons had chosen sides and we weren't on theirs) it did nothing to assuage the furious reaction I'd had to the fact my jerk cousin Robert and his viciously monstrous girlfriend, Rose, were going to see Alicia in her dress.

And. I. *Wasn't.*

Oh, Fee. So irrational. Yes, admittedly. About as irrational as my mother when it came to *my* wedding. So there.

I made it to the other side of the yard without being spotted, though there were several paddocks where riders cantered over jumps, observed by other breeched and helmeted folks who seemed intent on what was going on in front of them and, thankfully, ignored the fact a strange redheaded woman with what had to be a rather fixated look on her face marched through their midst.

It was still a fair hike to the main building, up a long lane, past what had to be housing for the riders. Why hadn't I just picked a closer tree, a nearer stretch of fence? I had no idea, even, what time the wedding was going to happen, only knowing that sometime in the next hour or so two people I cared about were going to tie the knot and I wasn't allowed to watch it happen.

Why, exactly, did I care? I wished I knew. Though perhaps the burning desire inside me to have Robert catch me here had something to do with it. What did I have to prove, anyway? Nothing. Though I actually caught my breath while a faintly hysterical—and maniacal, if I was going to be completely honest—giggle at the thought of my cousin even trying to arrest me burbled its presence while I shoved it down under an attempt at control.

Oh, what fun would be had. What fun, indeed. Ever since Crew's attempt to have Robert fired in June had failed, my cousin's boldness, his arrogance, had only grown in stature, along with his sagging gut and that disgusting creature on his upper lip that was surely a dying caterpillar and not human hair. Was that what this was really about? A chance to challenge that most despicable of human beings?

No. No, damn it. This was about friendship and family and the fact there was something dirty, rotten and truly dark going down in my town and I had been cut out of it with surgical precision.

Nosy? You betcha.

I was so lost in my thoughts, in my intense need to defy the Patterson ban on all things Fiona Fleming, I made a calculated error. Oh, hell, who am I kidding? I was that lost in my own head I really deserved what I got, picking bold brazen over erring on the side of caution. Regardless, I took full responsibility for what followed because there was no one else to blame.

As I approached the far side of the large courtyard and its ridiculous fountain, I failed to notice a rider approaching before it was too late. She noticed me, though, didn't she? And when she pulled her tall, black mare to a halt, I almost jumped, a meep escaping at the sight of the pair of them towering over me. Made worse when her eyes widened, and her eyebrows arched just as she spoke.

"I know you," she said. "You're Fiona Fleming."

Whoops.

CHAPTER TWO

I expected to be booted immediately, or at least called out for my presence. Surely the look the young rider gave me told me she knew exactly the state of affairs surrounding my identity and my illegal presence on the premises. Instead, she smiled, offering one hand, strong as I shook it in too much shock not to react on instinct.

"I've heard a lot about you," she said like we'd met casually and not during my lowest moment of criminal enterprise. "My aunt speaks very highly of you."

Aunt? It took me a second to make the connection, to pair the dark brown eyes with ones familiar already, to note the blonde bun pinned under the rim of her black velvet helmet, the shape of her cheekbones, lips, jawline. Even her build and the way she carried herself as she retrieved her hand, using it to pat the neck of the mare next to her, the giant creature bobbing her head and snorting, one large hoof impacting the ground in a thud of protest at being forced to stand still.

"You're Pamela Shard's niece?" Weird, I had no idea Pamela had family. Then again, it wasn't like we were on regular speaking terms these days, but had she ever mentioned a sibling with a daughter…?

"Sarah Shard," she nodded to me. "Aunt Pam is a big fan." She glanced over her shoulder, grimacing. "Though, I'm not so sure she's as happy about the family she married into."

Well now. Was this then a source of some insider information I previously lacked? I jumped on the opportunity to dig for details without thinking things through. Wedding? What wedding? Yeah, so the real reason I was there reared its ugly head and I hugged it tight like an addict needing her fix.

"I haven't talked to your aunt in a few months," I said, knowing it likely sounded a little whiny but pushing on anyway. "I've been worried about her." Okay, that at least emerged from my lips as genuine and heavy with real concern. Enough Sarah shrugged, glancing back yet again as if she expected to be chastised for speaking up.

"Me too," she admitted. "She and my dad might not have gotten along, brother and sister or not, but I've adored her since I was a kid." Sarah shifted her stance in her tall, leather boots, the gravel underfoot crunching. "You didn't warrant an invite to the wedding?"

Maybe she had no idea of the truth of things. I wasn't about to fill her in. "You know small towns," I said, doing my best to laugh it off and failing miserably at not being weird about it. "Politics."

Her nose wrinkled while she soothed her horse one more time. "I wouldn't know," she said. "Grew up in Boston. Though I can tell you the horse community is pretty small. So maybe I do know." Her laugh sounded enough like Pamela's, I caught myself laughing with her, even as my heart tightened against the feeling I was missing out on my friend's life. Regret, Fee. That was regret jerking hard on your emotions.

I wanted to ask a million questions—who, me? Ask questions of total strangers uninvited and without cause?—but we were interrupted by a second rider who joined us so quickly I didn't get a chance to even feel nervous about this additional witness to my break and entering activity.

The handsome young man made no bones about how he looked Sarah up and down, grinning at her and nodding to me, though his entire focus seemed pinned on the attractive blonde beside me. She ignored him for the most part, and I couldn't miss the eye roll she did her best to disguise while he spoke.

"Great ride out there, Sarah," he said. "SuSu was fantastic. You handle her like you two were meant for each other."

"Thanks, Jimmy," she said, patting the horse one more time. The big mare's dark brown eyes blinked slowly, nostrils flaring as she inhaled the scent from Sarah's offered fingers. "She's a great girl. I'm lucky to get to ride her."

"She's not yours?" I almost kicked myself for interrupting, wishing I'd kept my mouth shut. Way to make myself noticeable and everything. Like standing out in the open the way I was, doing nothing to actually pursue my clandestine goal of hunting down the bride and stalking her until I got to see her dress in person. While, apparently, wanting much more to dig up details as to the wrongdoing I was positive lurked in the Patterson compound.

Sarah didn't seem to mind, though Jimmy did frown slightly, the handsome brunette's matching brown eyes narrowing at me just slightly. Interfering with his mating ritual, was I? Huh. Didn't expect to feel suddenly protective of the young woman I'd just met, but our mutual connection to Pamela seemed to be all my heart and mind needed to spike my instincts.

"Sotheby Suzette belongs to the Pattersons," Sarah said. "I could never afford her myself." That sounded like real regret. "Fortunately, thanks to my invitation to join the center to train, I get to ride horses of her caliber in prep for my Olympic trial run."

"You'll nail your qualifier," Jimmy said, soft tenor pleasant enough but the leer he was giving her making my maternal drive simmer below the surface.

Wait. My what?

Sarah shrugged, though I noted the faint blush in her cheeks and realized then it wasn't standoffishness that kept her from returning his notice and attention. It was nerves, plain and simple. As attractive as Sarah was, had she really spent her whole life focused on horses and avoiding guys? Made me all the more Momma Bear.

Dear god. Was I really thinking with my uterus at a time like this?

"Are you also competing?" I chose to engage this young upstart in a conversation to give Sarah time to collect herself. Her brief, thankful look told me I'd pegged her while my heart constricted for her. I'd been where she was, a gangling redheaded girl with a big mouth who had no idea what to do with the young men who hit on her. Though I'd lost that sense of discomfort in high school and Sarah had to be in her early twenties. Maybe her discipline and focus on her riding goals had taken priority.

"I am." He smiled then, easily, flashing perfect white teeth, tan even and attractive, shoulders broad but body lean, a natural athlete in his breeches and boots. "James Hogan." He extended his hand, shook mine, without the intense pressure I'd been expecting, just firm and warm. Okay, maybe he wasn't so bad. Sarah could do worse. "But everyone calls me Jimmy."

Charming. I did an internal headshake and got a grip. Was I matchmaking for Pamela's niece while trying not to get caught breaking into the wedding I'd been pointedly not invited to? Yes. Yes, I was. Because Fiona Fleming never did anything halfway.

"Jimmy, Bronc is ready for you." Wow, I was losing my focus, clearly, my lack of attention to detail meaning yet another person joined us before I could make a clean getaway. This guy was older, maybe in his early thirties, like me, short, dark blond hair almost buzzed, his hazel eyes locking on me a moment while he frowned and paused. "Can we help you, ma'am?" I could see him stiffen as he took me in. Trust issues? Well, I had my own so I could hardly blame him. And, after all, I was committing a crime. Still put my back up, though, when he looked at me like that. "This is a restricted area."

"She's with me, Charlie," Sarah said, instantly, with so much calm self-assurance I almost forgot this was the same young woman who could barely take a bit of flirting from a handsome guy her age. Honestly, she surprised me with her choice to back my presence, her private wink almost triggering a grin I could barely contain.

This wasn't fun. Wasn't. Really.

The man she'd called Charlie wasn't dressed like her and Jimmy, his shorter, stockier frame draped in a dark blue coverall, gloves dangling from one pocket, rubber boots flecked with straw. He worked here?

"You know you're supposed to clear visitors with Melina." He didn't sound argumentative, though, backing down.

Sarah's sunny smile seemed to do the trick.

"Sorry, Charlie. Fiona came to meet SuSu."

I reached out, hesitant, encouraged by Sarah's nod, and touched the mare's soft nose. Okay, so I'd met a few horses in the past, was a fan of the gigantic and mostly gentle creatures I'd encountered, even ridden one or two in the kind of safe environment that included someone holding the reins while I held on for dear life. But this was an entirely different experience. The black mare turned her head toward me, hot breath washing over my skin, raising goosebumps on my arm as she delicately mouthed my fingertips before sighing heavily and shaking her head. The carefully braided folds of her short mane bounced on her glossy neck, that impatient hoof stamping one more time while Sarah laughed.

"She wants her cooldown and turnout," she said. "And she's earned it."

I had no idea what that meant, but nodded anyway, now thinking about my exit strategy. Maybe Sarah could help me maneuver my way deeper into enemy territory? I wasn't above using her for my own purposes, protective of her or not.

But I didn't get to leave just yet, not when the noisy clatter of another large horse entering the courtyard interrupted while we all turned to find a tiny brunette, her delicate features and dainty figure rather comical in comparison, jerking hard on the reins of a massive white horse who seemed intent on barreling right toward us.

CHAPTER THREE

I pictured a set of ten-pins crashing hard under the crushing weight of a bowling ball, frozen in place by the surge of fear I felt at impending doom on four hooves snorting and prancing its way toward me. But when no one else ran for the hills, I could, at least, be grateful to my lack of flight instinct that kept me from looking like a total coward.

Turned out this sort of thing was to be expected in the horse world. Who knew? Somehow, the itty-bitty little girl (she looked like she couldn't have been more than twelve) perched on the back of the giant creature had the upper hand. Despite the fact her horse had, at the very least, a mind of its own and surely wanted to ensure its freedom from the clearly inadequate strip of metal in its mouth controlled by two thin lines of leather that would never do the job. And yet, as the deceptively strong (and rather fearless and clearly confidently skilled) girl wrangled the white beast into submission, I took a shaking breath and a moment to be thankful it wasn't me in the horse's saddle.

Everyone standing in his path would have been toast.

Instead, she slapped him hard on the neck as he came to an abrupt halt, his long tail thrashing, foam falling in chunks from his mouth as he worked the bit, ears flat against his head. And while I'd initially been afraid of (what was now clearly a) him, and fearful for her, when she let out a long string of blistering swear words before hitting him hard with a short crop in her right hand, I had a sudden change of heart.

It took a special kind of person to piss me off. Temper or not, I could typically shrug off arrogance given enough time and distance. But there were particular activities that I couldn't let slide. Being mean to people I cared about? Check. Intentional cruelty or dishonesty? You betcha. And anyone who was harsh with animals?

Snarl.

Sure, he wasn't behaving himself, but there was no need, in my mind, to beat the poor creature. The brunette on the big, white gelding took zero care in her dismount, the poor creature's sides heaving as she'd obviously given him a massive workout and did little to wait for him to catch his breath before leaping from his back, one boot thudding against his side as she did, the reins tossed at Charlie as the young woman (and not a child after all upon close inspection), tiny beside the towering horse who spooked sideways in response, casually snapped the horse's nose with her gloves almost as an aside.

"He's being an absolute ass," she snarled at the stable hand. "Deal with it." She only then seemed to note Sarah and Jimmy stood there, with me as part of their little group. That triggered a shady little smirk at Jimmy and a rather suggestive hip cock before she fixed her nasty expression on Sarah.

"Saw you drop that last rail," she said. "Nice try." She snorted softly, delicately, cruel expression deepening while she tossed her head. "If you can't handle SuSu's power, maybe you should give her up, Sarah."

And, with that, whoever this young rider was succeeded in ticking every single box available to her.

I drew a breath to deliver some kind of scathing remark that would likely get me kicked out faster than the track I was already on, but Sarah was quicker. And, apparently, accustomed to the other woman's verbal assaults because she, unlike yours truly, kept her temper, even smiling, though the cutting tone of her voice spoke volumes.

"Jagger's time was off," she said, almost sweetly, right into the wide, bright blue eyes of her smaller counterpart. Fakes? Looked like contacts to me. "Not to mention you're mishandling him made him misbehave." The young woman stiffened at the criticism. Could dish but not eat her own crow? She needed a thicker skin. "Might want to keep an eye on the clock, Violet, not to mention your horse's manners." Sarah looked the girl up and down. "Oh. And your diet."

Wow. Did she just call the teensy-weensy rider in front of me fat? I gaped at Sarah, not sure how to feel about such an attack, as her rival's eyes narrowed into slits, the crop in her hand slapping her leg hard enough the giant horse beside her, now in Charlie's possession, snorted and shied once again. Telling me he was more than familiar with the strike of that stick she held. No wonder he was misbehaving. I'd be pissed at her too. Seeing his reaction was enough proof of abuse it cut off any kind of sympathy I might have had for Violet before it could grow.

Sarah wasn't done. "At least I'm riding consistently," she snapped then, snarled, really. One finger jabbed at the gelding whose head hung low, sides still heaving a little, body soaked with sweat. "And treating my horse with respect. When was the last time you were in the saddle? Two days ago? You might want to focus more on the trials, Violet, and less on dating and dinners out."

"Mind your own business," the tiny rider shot back. "Jagger's being an idiot. That's not my fault."

"Indeed." I spun, flinched at the sight of a tall, older man, now surrounded by breeches and golf shirts, though he wasn't helmeted. Thankfully, he ignored me and settled his scowling expression on Violet. "Miss Shard, if you don't mind." Sarah shrugged, looked away, Jimmy clearly uncomfortable, Charlie scowling, while the towering, barrel-chested man addressed Violet, not quite looming over her but close enough to call it what it was. "Miss Perry, pray tell me what you think that creature," he jabbed his index finger at the big, white horse, "has done to deserve being treated like some sort of mechanical instrument you can use up and toss away at your convenience?" His British accent, mild enough I missed it initially, heated up as he continued, becoming obvious that he might not have spent much time in the United Kingdom in the last twenty years or so, but his origins were more than obvious when his temper made an appearance.

Violet's petulance made itself known, arms crossing aggressively over her chest, the crop striking Charlie's arm before he could dodge. She didn't even acknowledge she'd hit him, scowling up at the man who'd just berated her while I realized we were drawing too much attention and I really, really needed to move on while the getting was good.

"He's acting out," she whined. "I told Melina, but she just got mad at me and insisted I keep riding him." Violet glared at Sarah. "I'm supposed to be on SuSu. You just got her because you're connected." Family, huh? Well, the Pattersons owned her, so there. Wait, was I on their side for some reason? Ew. Violet had returned her attention to the towering gentleman, facing him down like he wasn't more than twice her weight and easily a foot above her diminutive height. "Besides, you don't get to tell me what to do anymore, Alphonse," Violet shot her next volley. "I'm done wasting my talent on your worthless coaching."

Alphonse looked briefly uncomfortable, then angry himself. Felt weird to witness this clearly private bout of bitterness that the outside world didn't usually get to see. This wasn't my fight and I really had to go. I scanned quickly for a getaway plan, only to find myself cut off from moving forward by the mass of people I'd somehow found myself amidst, not to mention two hulking equine walls of fur and stomping feet. If I wanted to escape, I'd have to make myself conspicuous, circle around behind SuSu or cut through the argument.

Or retreat. And there was no way I was leaving until someone told me to.

"You arrogant little gnat." Alphonse's voice rang, a powerful tenor, echoing around the courtyard, drawing more attention from other riders who paused before scurrying away. So, this had to be a familiar battle people learned to avoid? Lucky me. "Why Melina continues to support your uselessness I have no idea." He sniffed. "You're lack of skill and abusive behavior only creates stress in your mount. You have no one to blame but yourself. And your terrible choice in coaches."

Sarah eye-rolled at me. Yup. Ancient argument. One that drew out yet another body, this one with the authority, I could tell from her stomping step and the logo stitched into the fabric of her golf shirt, though she didn't notice me just yet. Instead, she stopped next to Violet who glanced at her with a flicker of guilt before the woman spoke, toe-to-toe with Alphonse.

"You are here as a courtesy," she said, hands on her hips, short, dark hair rather wild as if she'd just stripped off her own helmet. She'd held onto her youthful figure though she was older than me, lines around her eyes and mouth deeper than they should have been, tan telling me she'd spent her whole life in the sun, likely on the back of a horse. "But I've warned you before to stay away from my riders." She paused a moment before her voice dropped as she glanced sideways at Jagger. The tall gelding still danced in Charlie's hands, clearly unhappy with the level of tension around him. Well, high strung I understood. He was clearly an athlete and stressed out. Melina took note herself, it seemed, spinning back to Alphonse with fury on her face. "And their horses."

"Alphonse Brunbaugh goes where he wishes," he said, drawing himself up to his impressive height and towering over her much as the two equines in our midst towered over the rest of us, "and does what he chooses." He sniffed at Sarah, gestured at SuSu. "I'm merely pointing out to you and your protégé," he said that word like it was an insult, "her failure will be on her. And you, Melina."

I was expecting the two of them to have a giant fight. Clearly, the grown adults were as unhappily competitive and confrontational as the young men and women they trained. I felt an unexpected surge of gratitude I'd grown up without the kind of pressure that had obviously shaped and evolved this small group of people into the angry, frustrated and in Violet's case, petulantly argumentative collection of souls I found myself shaking my head at.

Judging others. My favorite.

But it was Sarah who shocked me the most with her reaction to Melina. Her whole persona shifted, the sweet young woman I equated with the hard-assed but generally awesome Pamela Shard transforming from rather innocent if confident in her handling of her big horse to snarling animal ready to bite off its own leg if that was what she needed to do to win.

"I am *sick*," she was practically screaming, and she'd barely gotten started, "and *tired*," she lashed out with one hand toward Violet, almost striking Melina in the process, "of that *rider*," she was barely audible now, her horse stomping and snorting in fear, "trying to undermine *my* training." Holy Hannah. Pent up rage much? "And the next time she tries to interfere," Sarah shook her index finger in Melina's face while the older woman's expression darkened, her cheeks deep red, a vein I knew from the forehead of my own darling Crew leaping out in response to the verbal assault, "I'm taking this to the Olympic committee and having her banned."

"And I've had it," the coach snapped while Alphonse heaved a sigh and tried to get between them while Sarah actually lunged for Melina, the older woman's temper clearly frayed to the limit, "with your attitude, Miss Shard. You ride here because I allow it, and only because I allow it. That can change. In an instant." She snapped her fingers in Sarah's face.

Oh, boy. Coming from someone with a temper? Melina's challenge… accepted.

CHAPTER FOUR

So, I'd clearly walked in on an old fight, one that had the sort of fuse that could literally burst into an explosion without any kind of provocation an outsider could comprehend. If Sarah's expression in response was anything to go by, if Melina could die a horribly painful death by glare alone, she'd have been writhing on the ground then and there, howling her final breaths in agony and despair while Pamela's niece laughed over her suffering.

As for Alphonse, I wasn't really all that convinced he was there to help, to be honest, and his attempts to keep Sarah from physically attacking Melina seemed half-hearted at best. I was positive at any second it would come to blows and, though her temper and reaction shocked and horrified me, I was poised to leap in between the women and give keeping them apart a solid go despite the risk to my person if only because, despite everything, Pamela was my friend and friends helped out when they could.

But it seemed like no intent to do good went unpunished, at least for me in that particular circumstance. Because before I could stop Sarah from doing something she'd surely regret down the road while Violet smirked, Jimmy stood by with his hands in his pockets and Charlie scowled at the continuing agitation of the white horse whose reins he held tightly in his fist, two further additions to the unfolding drama made themselves present and accounted for, though it was the tall, broad-shouldered woman, not the even taller and stunningly handsome blond man in the suit at her side who broke up the show.

My brain told me I knew this guy from somewhere, the angular gorgeousness of his face remarkable, the intensity of his blue eyes. How he carried himself with casual confidence, yummy beyond measure. Sure, I was in love with Crew, but this was the kind of man who could fire up hormones in a corpse.

Fee. Focus. Where had I seen him before? And more importantly, how was I going to escape this mess and continue my quest to witness Alicia's wedding when I was now fully hemmed in by these people and their disastrous relationships that had nothing to do with me?

I know what you're thinking. I'd spent my entire time back home in Reading poking my nose in, being a busybody and generally making a pain in the butt of myself when it came to other people's problems. Paying the piper, hens coming home to roost, karma and all that, I got it, I really did. Just, did my penchant for being in the middle of conflict have to ruin my current plans so effectively?

"Enough, Sarah. Melina." The big woman's upper right arm bore an embroidered name, identifying her as Gretchen Latrell, facility manager. She glanced my way as I did my best to be inconspicuous, her eyes narrowing at the sight of me. "My office, now. As for you, Miss Fleming," Gretchen's scowl turned to a flare of nervous anxiety before she returned to her show of force, "you're here without permission."

Sarah didn't even try to defend me this time and fair enough. Looked like she had her own problems. I shrugged, crossing my arms over my chest, going for my own brand of confident nonchalance while the big blond at her side cocked his head in my direction, his frown doing nothing to shake out the memory of our previous meeting.

"I'm here for the wedding," I said, going for a bluff despite knowing it was a lost cause. She knew who I was which meant she'd been informed I wasn't to be allowed anywhere near the nuptials Didn't stop me from trying, though. "Got lost. Sorry about that. I'll just be on my way."

Gretchen wasn't buying it. Wait, where did those two security guards come from? Big boys in black outfits and guns strapped to their thighs, ball caps pulled low over their Neanderthal foreheads, they seemed to appear out of nowhere though, I did mention my focus was off, right? Likely they'd been lurking, and I'd missed them. "Please escort Miss Fleming off the property." Her cold, hazel eyes never left mine. "If I catch you in the facility again, I'm pressing charges. Are we clear?"

Grumble. Mumble. Fine.

That's how I found myself firmly deposited outside the main gate of the equestrian center, those two security guards watching me as I plodded my way across the parking lot, past a handful of guests in afternoon wedding attire heading in the opposite direction, head down, hands in pockets, almost ready to admit defeat.

Almost.

Stubborn, I know. It was a long, slow walk to where I'd stashed my car, the mid-September early afternoon heat cut in part by the towering tree shadowing the interior. Still, it was warm enough inside I was sweating after a few minutes of sitting with my hands clutching the steering wheel, my jaw aching from my clenched teeth, slow burn of anger bubbling like lava ready to erupt in my chest.

I couldn't leave. But I couldn't stay. Now what?

My brain, seeking a distraction, went to the man with Gretchen and, as I scowled over memories long buried, I made a connection in part thanks to the dangling heart keychain Daisy had given me as a silly engagement present. It sat on the passenger's seat as if challenging me to march back inside and not take no for an answer.

I leaped at the distraction as his name surfaced in my head. Emile Reis, right? That was it. No, it wasn't lost on me I couldn't ever seem to remember any of my staff by their first names but a hot, tall blond I'd met once almost three years ago? Him I remembered.

Daisy had been the one to introduce me, of all people. Some kind of European investor Olivia lured here. Speaking of Daisy, she'd been on his arm on Valentine's Day, almost three years ago, hadn't she? At the White Valley Lodge. The same night Mason Patterson was murdered.

But wait, he'd ended up with Vivian, I seemed to recall. So maybe he wasn't so hot after all.

Huh. Okay, little mystery solved. Big deal. Honestly, figuring out his identity just left me more frustrated. The fact who amounted to pretty much a stranger from another freaking continent was allowed behind those vaulted freaking walls and I freaking wasn't...

My phone rang and I ignored it, mainly because I wasn't in the headspace to talk to anyone but also because it was my father and he really, really didn't want to hear what I had to say right then. The second time it rang, and Crew's face popped up I freed my right hand long enough to toss the stupid thing across the car where it impacted the window before landing with a thud on the passenger's side floor.

It stopped ringing. And chimed. I glared at the screen, still lit, the phone landing face-up and the accusing text from my fiancé only fueling my fire.

Please tell me you're not at the wedding.

Argh.

Fee, I love you. Please, if you are at the wedding, go home. I'm begging you. Stay out of it.

A sudden flood of calm washed over me, the sort of out-of-body release of endorphins that told me I was about to make a terrible, terrible decision and couldn't care less. Surely my darling sweetheart, the love of my life, had to know sending those texts put a giant GO lit in green and sparkles front and center? He might as well have shaken a red cape at a raging bull.

Right. Because blaming Crew Turner for what I was about to do made all the sense in the world.

The fence beckoned. I picked another stretch of it, heaved myself over, and this time managed to escape the bulk of the riders and security's attention as I hustled my way across the compound. I did suffer one slight setback as I neared the main administrative building for the riders, hearing shouting out an open window and pausing long enough to see Gretchen, Melina and Charlie fighting over something in the manager's office, but they were yelling over each other and, honestly, I'd learned my lesson.

Minding my own business. For the time being. Until I saw Alicia's dress. Then all bets were off.

The fight had them sufficiently occupied and sent everyone scurrying so the incident I'd previously considered a negative turned into a positive. Instead of drawing attention, it seemed the massive shouting battle had given me the all-clear I needed to navigate my way to success. I was almost chortling with delight at my cleverness and tenacity as I hurried up the long, paved lane toward the larger facility where I imagined fluffy white perfection awaited, positive I was on the brink of achieving my goal this time with no one to stop me.

No one, that was, except for the lurking security guards who sent me scrambling for hiding places every freaking two seconds. I spent the following twenty minutes or so dodging from tree to tree, even falling face-first into a ditch to avoid detection from the persistence of the Patterson's attempt to keep me from the wedding. Okay, so assuming all the guards were for my benefit was clearly overkill on my part and a bit arrogant, truth be told. It became apparent even to me in my heightened state of hell no you're not keeping me from what I want that the level of security engaged for this event was a bit excessive, even for the Pattersons.

And I found myself wondering, as I huddled inside the open end of a large culvert, grimacing at the dirty water covering my sneakers while two guards chatted over my head, just what it was they were guarding against.

I was finally forced to retreat back toward the stables, debating my next step, when I spotted him and everything I'd done up to now flew out the window. Robert was dressed in uniform, my arrogant and annoying cousin's gut pushing against the buttons of his khaki shirt, the two guards he spoke to frowning at him as he rambled on, far enough away I wasn't graced with the details of his instructions but close enough to see the clear disdain the rental cops held him in.

Well, they weren't all bad then, were they? But no way was I getting caught by Robert Carlisle of all people. That would just be the very end of an extremely crappy and frustrating caper I would never, ever live down.

Just my luck, he turned and headed my way, forcing me to dodge into the stable and the dark humidity of the heavy air. I heard his footfalls approach, heart pounding in time. He must have spotted me, was in pursuit. No, I couldn't go down like this, not today. Not ever. But with my escape cut off, the far exit shut tight and latched, I had no choice but to slip into a stall, pulling the door shut behind me, crouching behind it in the hope he wouldn't find me, knowing I was now trapped and had zero options left.

Panic jerked against my nerves and, when his footfalls stopped outside my stall door, I choked on it. Not that Robert scared me, not in the least. Except, for a moment, I found myself inexplicably locked in memory, standing on a dock, soaking wet and holding Vivian French in my arms, while a looming shadow hovered and the childhood terror of watching Victor drown overwhelmed me.

CHAPTER FIVE

It must have been the intensity of my emotions that made the old history surface, like a short in my brain that carried me to the most horrifying and terrifying experience of my young life. Since I'd only recently recovered the memory, it had equally more and less impact on me than had it been with me my whole life. More, in the sense that it was still fresh enough feeling I was continuing to gather details and less because, I think, if I'd been forced to suffer through it for more than the length of time I had now, as an adult, it might have driven me mad.

Still might. Jury was out at the moment.

But it did mean I was able to get control over the images and smoosh them down. My mind was used to doing it, after all, spent a little over two decades hiding it from me and as I inhaled a shaking breath, anxious nerves clenching around my throat, Robert spoke, dispelling the last of the return to childhood and that terrible day.

"I'm here," he said. "What do you need?"

It took a long moment for me to realize he wasn't speaking to me. Long enough for the person he'd obviously come to meet to answer in a low, soft voice I didn't recognize.

"You've been spending far too much time of late focusing on what doesn't matter." A woman's voice, deeper than most, with the faintest hint of disdain despite the level and lovely tone of it. I actually would have quite liked to sit and listen to her tell me a story or two over tea, if it weren't for the fact she was clearly in cahoots with my obnoxiously gross cousin. She was older, I guessed, her words measured as if she spent a lot of time on enunciation and precision. Reminded me somewhat of my dearly departed Grandmother Iris. Huh, wasn't expecting to make that connection at all. As the nervous panic faded into curiosity so powerful, I was shaking all over again but for a different reason, I barely resisted the urge to pop my head up enough to take a peek at the stranger while Robert answered.

"It's not my fault," he grumbled in his ever-so-pathetic way, all kicked puppy to her collected and slightly stilted speech, though sounding like she'd berated him down to the ground despite the fact she'd barely chastised him as far as I'd heard. "It's Turner and Fanny. Not to mention Uncle John—"

"Your typical excuses are, as always, a waste of my time, Robert." This time she sounded almost bored, tired. So, she was as underwhelmed by him as I was? Fair enough and, under different circumstances, might have been sufficient to make us friends. And yet, I was deep into suspicions of who she might be and knew to the bottom of my soul no matter what happened or who she called bosom buddy long and ever ago, she and I would always be on opposite sides. "I need the meddling taken care of. You understand how important it is, don't you? That we are allowed to proceed with our plans unhindered?" The sound of a soft tread, the barest whisper of fabric. Was she approaching him? Her voice was even lower, closer, when she went on. "I'm doing my part, Robert, dear. As are others. Putting the right amount of pressure where required, the proper level of barriers between us and those who would oppose us." Insidious, her tone, her perfectly reasonable words with the faintest hint of warmth returning like she cared about him when I was positive if she was who I thought she was, she had no idea what real caring actually was. "Not just for the family, Robert. But your own peace of mind. We both know how important it is certain facts remain among just us if we're to ensure each other's safety and our success."

There was nothing really damning in her statements, her questions, her coercive sweetness. So why then did I feel like I needed a shower? That she'd drizzled me with honey laced with the acridest poison known to man?

"I swear, I'll take care of it." Why did he sound so afraid? My guesses had evolved into solid choices, positive now I knew to whom it was he spoke, but their proximity held me in place, frustration growing. Just say something, anything, that I could use, some actual incriminating statement and not this sideways hinting at what I really needed to know. All it would take was one single usable fact and I'd have them both.

No such luck, apparently.

"I'm certain of it," the woman said, her tone brightening further, even jocular, bordering on kind and grandmotherly. I shivered in response, goosebumps rising on my arms as I accepted, I was in the presence of pure evil, the kind of darkness that devoured with a pretense of love and conviction hiding the blackest of hearts. "I have every faith in you, Robert. As always."

Wow, she was either blind to the fact he was a total failure and a waste of breath, or she was humoring him. Surely, she knew he wasn't worthy of her trust? Of course, she was. The woman I suspected stood on the other side of the stall door wasn't a fool. She had to be using him as bait or a distraction or just another line of defense to keep me from her gates.

Regardless of her motives, he spluttered a moment before answering, his own voice filled with relief and a level of gratitude one reserved for someone who owned their soul.

"You can count on me."

There was a long silence before she sighed. "We really should be going, Robert. I wouldn't want to miss the wedding."

He grunted and I could actually picture him standing there with his mouth hanging open like a useless ape. No, wait. That was insulting apes, wasn't it? His footsteps retreated in a hurry, and I almost exhaled in relief. Until I realized I hadn't heard her leave just yet.

So, I'd been in some pretty tight situations in the past, felt my heartbeat race to the point I was sure it would give in on me and just shrug itself into oblivion because of fear. But I'd never, ever, in my life felt the kind of growing panic leading to hyperventilation and imminent expiration from utter terror as I did in that moment. I had no idea why it was I felt such fear, why it grasped me firmly in both hands and squeezed me so hard I was positive this was it, the end of Fiona Fleming, crouched and inconsequential in the grand scheme of whatever was going on in my town, behind the dirty stall door of a horse's house. And still, the woman didn't move, didn't even seem to breathe, though the pounding of my pulse in my ears could easily have blotted out any sound of her moving, inhaling, exhaling while I held my own breath and darkness closed in around the edges of my vision while my body begged me for fresh oxygen.

Her footfalls finally retreated, hurried and firm and I gasped, collapsing sideways against the closed door, tears pricking the corners of my eyes, the need to pant out my panic clenching my chest into a knot of pressure powerful enough to make my lungs cramp.

And still, the good old Fleming curiosity won out, didn't it? Because just as sunlight flashed and the creak of a distant door caught my attention I lurched upward, only fast enough to catch the sight of her retreating back, of her pale blue dress, coiffed gray hair, the pearls around her neck as the sunlight illuminated her before the door she exited slipped shut behind her.

I sank once more to the floor, hand on my thudding heart, breathing through my mouth, my feet stuck out in front of me, not caring I was likely sitting in horse crap as the straw crinkled around me.

I had no proof. I'd never seen her before in my life. But I had zero doubt in that moment the woman who I'd overheard, the very one I'd caught a glimpse of, was none other than Marie Patterson herself.

Who had something on my cousin Robert, something she was leveraging to get him to… what? Distract me, Crew, Dad? Get rid of us? The idea that Robert had an agenda wasn't new, though any ability he had to follow through on such an order had always been kind of laughable considering how useless he was. And yet, with Rose at his side, that hideously clever half-sister of my beloved Daisy? The addition of that particular thorny bramble had upped Robert's game considerably.

And I now had proof of a sort—earwitness if not

eyewitness—that the Pattersons were controlling my cousin, were even ordering him to interfere with… no. I lowered my face into my hands, feeling the fine sheen of sweat that had broken out on my skin, dabbing at it with the cuff of my shirt while I pulled myself together. No proof of anything except that Robert and who I could only guess was Marie talked about something I couldn't even specifically identify.

My temper rose in a wash of heat that drove me to my feet, fists clenched at my sides while the reason I'd come here in the first place faded into the background and my fury at being manipulated by someone I couldn't hold accountable took over.

I might not have had any details yet. But now that I had my own version of evidence something truly shady was going on and that Marie Patterson was behind it (just try and convince me otherwise), nothing would stop me from getting to the bottom of whatever it was she was doing to my town.

Dad. Crew. Me. We were in her way, were we? Well, we'd see what we could do to ramp up our pesky ways and make her play her cards out in the open. Sure, I had zero idea what it was she was actually after, but I knew a few players I could lean on.

I hated being manipulated. But most of all, I absolutely, utterly and completely hated being afraid.

As I turned to leave the stall, my foot hit something soft and yet firm enough to stir the pile of straw I'd been huddled in. I looked down, annoyed by the interruption to my intended exit and froze, a faint groan exiting my lips.

Damn it. Not now. Why me?

I couldn't bring myself to feel bad for the owner of the limp, pale hand sticking up out of the bedding, not even when I crouched with a long-suffering sigh and, using a twig that had been part of the horse's floor covering, brushed aside enough of the golden straw to look down into the staring eyes of Melina Canty.

You know you've found too many dead bodies in your lifetime when uncovering one becomes rather a bother and more than a bit blasé. Not that I was minimalizing the death of the riding coach, but... yeah. I had bigger issues to deal with. I actually considered nipping out and letting someone else deal with the mess, to be honest. Because seriously, I was so over the whole stumbling over murder and mayhem when my town, my family and my love were at some shadowed risk I didn't even understand yet.

Except, of course, I was John Fleming's daughter and, though I debated that sneaky exit in favor of leaving the dirty work to others, I couldn't bring myself to let some poor stable hand live through the nightmares that surely would follow uncovering the woman's dead body. Considering I had lots of experience with said bad dreams, it was only fair I do my civic duty and shoulder this burden.

Though, as I stood with my hands on my hips, scowling at the ground while my friend, Deputy Jill Wagner, took my statement, I caught myself second-guessing my choice in the matter.

Made worse, as I recounted the edited version of why I was in the stall in the first place—no way I was fessing up to eavesdropping on the clandestine conversation with Robert lurking nearby, listening with that disgusting facial hair of his wriggling around as if in the throes of some horrible seizure. Let him wonder what I'd heard, how much and if I knew exactly who it was he'd been talking to. I glared at him when I finished giving my statement, just as the distant, sweet strains of the wedding march reached me from somewhere past the main office.

Insult, meet injury. Thanks for playing.

Jill's sympathetic smile wasn't helping any. Nor did her whispered question that had nothing to do with the case. "Why do you care so much? After the way they treated you?"

Why indeed? Because the kids were my friends, damn it. Now more than ever, as I thought about the conversation I'd overheard, as I stared death at my cousin, as I clenched myself against the need to screech in frustration, I believed Jared and Alicia, Pamela and Aundrea, the people I cared about were under the evil, controlling influence of Marie Patterson.

My Flemingness wouldn't stand for leaving one single soul behind. Until they told me otherwise, until someone I actually adored and admired and loved informed me I was wrong about Marie, and likely even then, I would not give up until I knew what the hell was going on.

Jill's phone rang, saving her the biting reply I was formulating, and she answered it hastily as if knowing she'd asked the wrong question at the worst time imaginable. "Sheriff," she said, eyes locked on mine. "Yes, she's right here."

And, awesome. Crew, right on cue. A car pulled up, gravel crunching under the tires, while Jill continued her conversation. I glanced at the new arrivals as she spoke, not surprised to see Geoffrey Jenkins emerge from the dark sedan, nor Mayor Olivia Walker, finally joined by Robert who chose then—now that he had others to use as an excuse to interrupt—to saunter along behind them. The pair joined me, and Jill's voice dropped when she turned away to finish her talk with her boss.

"Fee." Olivia looked like she held her fury in a barely contained bubble she'd perfected during her years as a politician, though I could tell she was at the breaking point. Then again, the mayor of Reading was always at her breaking point, so nothing new there. Still, not like her to use my nickname in an official capacity.

"Olivia." I nodded to her, ignoring Geoffrey whose shark-like demeanor hadn't changed one little bit. It had been a while since we'd crossed paths, but he was still the watchful predator I'd learned to despise when he did his best to oust the woman standing next to him from the mayor's office.

"You need to go." Olivia actually reached out and grasped my elbow with one manicured hand, her pale peach nail polish matching her pant suit, the perfect curves of her short nails digging into my skin through the fabric of my shirt. I was so startled by her act and her demand I almost let her drag me toward the car, pulling back at the last second, my own anger flaring all over again.

"You don't get to tell me what to do." Weird. Olivia was always on my side. I'd had her back, hadn't I? Endlessly. And yet, as she glared at me, I realized her own anger wasn't aimed at the usual background noise I figured she had to deal with but instead was laser-focused on yours truly.

What the actual...? What changed?

Olivia didn't get to comment, not when Jill spun toward me, her face pale, eyes wide, as she held out the cell phone in her hand, and Crew's deep, graveled voice interrupted, silencing everyone as if he stood there in person.

"Fiona Fleming," he said, "I hereby deputize you as an official member of the Reading Sheriff's Department and command you, in my absence, to assist Deputy Wagner in this investigation."

CHAPTER SIX

I gaped at the phone in Jill's hand while my deputy friend shot me a wry grin that told me she knew this announcement was coming, likely had been warned by the man I loved a moment before he told his employee to put him on speakerphone and make me the center of unhappy attention.

Thing was, the instant he made his announcement, the fury on Olivia's face flashed to relief and, without missing a beat, she stuck her hand out to me and shook my limp and unresponsive one while she pumped away at my arm like I'd been waiting my whole life for this accolade.

"Welcome to the team, Fiona," she said, nodding abruptly like she'd only then made up her mind about me and hadn't cajoled, canoodled and conspired her way into my sort of if not completely good graces time and time again. "I'm sure with your talent and expertise this horrible incident will be behind us in short order."

Geoffrey's unhappy expression spoke volumes, but he didn't argue or speak, choosing instead to back down with a narrowing of his eyes for Olivia and a short nod for me. Obviously, there was some kind of power play ongoing between the two of them, something I wasn't privy to, and might never uncover the truth of at this rate. The fact my fiancé chose to ruffle the kind of feathers that put Olivia's support in my wheelhouse all over again did little to elevate my mood, though I doubted my mood was at the top of Crew's list. Then again, knowing him as well as I did, maybe how I was feeling was exactly where his brain settled.

Olivia gestured at the phone still perched in Jill's hand as if Crew could see her. "You'll be returning, Sheriff Turner, in short order, I assume?"

"I'm tied up for the moment," he said. "But I shouldn't be much longer." Now I wanted to know where he'd went and why, seeing as the distraction of the wedding's siren call was over with. Because it was all about me, thank you. "In the meantime, if I could talk to my deputies, please. In private."

Olivia grunted like he'd handed her a sour candy when she was expecting sugar, taking a moment to lean into me, her pale painted lips near my ear. "You're on, Fee," she whispered. "But it's the last time I can protect you." She actually sounded exasperated. "For heaven's sake, would you stop finding dead bodies!" She turned then and strode off, back toward the car, Geoffrey sparing one last look for me before joining the mayor, with a rather pointed stare for Robert on his way past.

My cousin didn't join us when Jill closed ranks with me, the phone between us, Crew's voice carrying more than I'd like despite the fact Robert seemed to take zero interest in what the sheriff was saying.

"Crew," I said, keeping my voice down, "we need to talk. There's more I haven't said."

"Later," he answered. "When I'm back in Reading. For now, follow Jill's lead and Fee." He sounded pained, under strain. "Are you okay?"

Sigh. "I'm fine," I said, hating how ordinary this felt. A woman was dead, after all, someone I'd just met, who had stood next to me, breathing and arguing and very much alive not so long ago. Where was my compassion? And my curiosity? "Can I ask what you were thinking just now?"

I didn't have to see the man I loved to know he was eye-rolling and likely suppressing a huge sigh. "You've proven in the past you're just going to investigate anyway," he said. "And have made yourself useful." Wow, a bit begrudging even for him. "Besides, at least this way I know where you are and what you are doing so I can keep an eye on you." The fact I'd had my life threatened and came close to death about as many times as I'd stumbled on an already dead body was likely right at the top of his mind, so fair enough. "Just stick close to Jill and follow her advice. Okay?"

Grunt. "I already have a few angles to investigate." I raised my eyebrows at Jill who shrugged.

"Deputy Wagner, please take the lead." Was Crew saying that for Robert's benefit? He sounded pretty official, and while I wasn't surprised—come on, she was the real deputy after all, since I had zero illusions about my position being in name only and applied for reasons I'm sure Crew was going to share with me before long. "I'll be back in town shortly. I want a full report when I arrive."

"Yes, sir, Sheriff." Jill took him off speaker, raising the phone to her ear. I heard Crew's voice again, thin and distant before she nodded and hung up, sliding the slim cell into her back pocket and then grinning at me suddenly like this whole scenario ticked her funny bone as nothing else ever had. "Finally," she said, voice barely above a whisper. "Welcome to the team officially, Fee."

I watched the sedan pull away, the music over, knowing Olivia and Geoffrey missed the wedding because of me and doing my very best not to feel smug about it. While the mayor was clearly dealing with Patterson issues of her own, she'd been invited, hadn't she?

Nope, not bitter or anything.

"I hope you don't think this actually means you're welcome in this investigation, Fanny." Leave it to Robert to assume anything he said was important or valuable. I crossed my arms over my chest and glared as he bellied up to the conversation, hauling at the sagging belt loops of the jeans he wore as the lower half of his uniform, snuffling before spitting off to one side in a revolting show of just how classless he really was. If anything embodied Robert Carlisle's disgusting insides it was the glob of phlegm that came so unpoetically into the light, a vile reminder his outsides weren't much better.

Just. Gross.

"Deputy Carlisle," Jill spoke up before I had the chance to tell Robert where to shove all the crap I had to give up the teensy weensy crack of his nonexistent butt. "You mentioned earlier you thought you saw an intruder, that you were investigating just that possibility when Fee called in the body?"

Robert looked like she'd handed him something that smelled worse than the horse manure I'd been sitting in. "So?"

Jill shrugged, all casual and nonchalant despite the fact I knew her far better than Robert, apparently, because I had to fight a grin to keep from snorting my delight at what was coming. "Since Sheriff Turner told me to take lead, I'm going to need you to finish your search and then write up a report based on that investigation. So, we have all the avenues covered."

He glanced at me, still not getting the fact she was effectively sending him on a wild goose chase. Because either he a) lied about the search so she wouldn't know why he'd been in the barn's proximity or b) didn't want to admit he'd figured out I was the intruder he'd gone looking for and suspected I'd overheard his clandestine conversation. Regardless, he stammered around a comment while Jill turned her back on him.

"Now, Deputy Carlisle," she said, waving him off over one shoulder. "Deputy Fleming, shall we begin the interviews?"

Robert's flat, furious expression showed the darkness I'd become accustomed to when he felt truly and completely wronged. It scared me the first time and, if I was going to be honest, still sent shivers down my spine. That level of utter black, that depth of vibrating rage, told me one thing about my cousin—that I'd underestimated him for a long time and continued to, at least to a point. In those moments when the truth of his soul showed through, Robert allowed me to see he was capable of literally anything under the right set of pressures.

I was surprised when he didn't argue with Jill, instead turning and stalking off, shoulders bent, face a mask, kicking at the gravel at his feet. Petulance aside, there was something truly hideous about him that told me I had to start taking him seriously if only so I had an early warning system if he decided to finally snap.

I turned to Jill to bring her in on what I was thinking when we were interrupted by, to my surprise, the unhappy and uncomfortable Sarah Shard. She nodded to Jill who nodded back while giving over her attention to me. I hated recalling the fight not so long ago as I reached out and grasped her hand a moment before letting Sarah go. So weird to feel attached to her still, to think of Pamela at a time like this when, if I was going to be honest with myself, the most likely suspect stood right in front of me.

That was if Melina was murdered. Dr. Aberstock had, as yet, to confirm. So why then wasn't I thinking a body buried in straw in an empty stall had died of natural causes? Cynicism aside, I had little doubt the woman had been killed. Why remained to be uncovered.

"Thank you for defending me earlier." I tucked my hands into my back pockets to keep myself from reaching out to Sarah again. "I appreciate you trying to have my back."

Sarah's unhappiness faded a bit as she hugged herself, forced a tiny smile. "You're Aunt Pam's friend," she said. "It feels like I know you, Fee. She speaks so highly of you, all the time."

"Even now?" I flinched a bit, glanced at Jill who remained silent, watchful, unjudging.

Sarah looked confused. "I don't know what you mean. Did you two have a fight?" She sighed then. "I talked to her this morning, and she mentioned you."

Huh. "Your aunt hasn't spoken to me in ages," I said. "She's been avoiding me." Why was I dragging Sarah into this? And so much for deputy duties. But Jill didn't alter my line of questioning or try to intervene, so I let Sarah answer.

"Honestly," the young rider said, voice dropping,

"you're not the only one. It's like pulling teeth trying to get Aunt Pam to talk these days." She glanced over her shoulder at Robert, then back to me. "Is something going on?"

So, she didn't know anything either. Craptastic. Rather than dig further into a line of questions that did nothing to serve the dead woman and only made me crazy, I grasped my need to know about things that had nothing to do with Sarah and pulled out the regularly scheduled playbook. "Sarah, I have to ask—"

My inquiry into her relationship with the victim had to wait, however. At least, until the furious intrusion of the violently verbal Violet Perry crashed our little question and answer. She grasped Sarah's arm, spun her around, tiny face dark red with rage as she jabbed a finger at the young woman I already thought of as a friend.

"Why haven't you arrested her?" Violet's shriek of accusation echoed back from the surrounding stables as if the whole place agreed with her. "Sarah killed Melina!"

CHAPTER SEVEN

Okay, so the thought had crossed my mind, too, but I wasn't about to accuse Pamela's niece of murder, quite to the contrary. I had been hoping to question her before anyone brought up the fight, though of course, my own personal needs had gotten in the way. Not feeling guilty about it or anything, especially when Robert took that as his signal to hustle forward with cuffs in hand, roughly jerking Sarah's arms behind her back to the sickening snick of the bracelets sliding home.

"I've heard enough," he said as if a single accusation was sufficient to make her a murderer. Sarah tried to protest but I knew better than to fight my cousin when he had that look on his face. "You're coming to the office for questioning."

I glanced at Jill, waiting for her to say something, to jump in and argue the cuffs weren't necessary, that taking her into the office was a bit of overkill when we'd barely had time to question anyone, let alone her or the now sniffling and rather satisfied Violet who refused to meet my eyes while Robert tugged on Sarah's upper arm with one ham hand, dragging her toward the cruiser parked nearby, lights still flashing.

But my deputy friend didn't fight the inevitable either, stepping out of Robert's way, while I met Sarah's eyes and nodded to her with what I hoped was a supportive expression and didn't simply make her regret knowing me in that moment. Whether she blamed me or not for her sudden arrest, I didn't know, falling silent after an initial, incoherently voiced complaint, sullenly ducking her head as he guided her into the back of his car. He saluted me and Jill, grinning like he'd gotten the upper hand on both of us, and drove off with his suspect while I exhaled slowly in an effort not to freak out and scream my frustration out at the top of my lungs.

"Everyone saw the fight." Violet's sudden comment made me turn back to her, note her flare of guilt. Over what? Calling Sarah out? Did she expect such an outcome or perhaps was just lashing out? Regardless, regret was pretty clear for the instant I registered it, before Violet shrugged, arms around herself, looking down and to the side before finishing her comment. "You were here, even. You know she did it."

I didn't, as a matter of fact. "I suppose Sarah was

the only person here to ever fight with Ms. Canty?" Wow, I sounded like Dad just then. Or maybe even Crew. I didn't have a badge, but clearly being deputized gave me the gravitas I'd been lacking previously. Either that, or my fiancé was finally wearing off on me.

Violet glared like she wished I hadn't brought that up. But I didn't get to push her further, not even for the sake of just poking at her, whether she had anything to do with the death of Melina or not. Because Geoffrey chose that moment to return in the same sedan, to exit the hastily stopped car, and to join us with a scowl on his normally cold face.

And he wasn't alone. Those two bulky security guards had joined him, black-clad forms tall and broad, bright yellow writing embroidered across their right biceps, dark sunglasses hiding their eyes. Now that I took the time to pay attention, something other than being ejected from the center to focus on, I realized they smelled suspiciously of retired military to me, so some kind of hired mercenary force, a private security firm? Why did that suddenly make me think of Blackstone Corporation and their shady dealings?

Because they didn't just smell like Blackstone. They stank.

"While Miss Fleming's new position remains in question," Geoffrey started.

"Deputy Fleming," Jill corrected him with cold confidence to rival his usual shark-like nature. They exchanged a long look, my friend not backing down even a hair, the red peaks of the Patterson family member's cheeks growing darker as he did his best to stand his own ground against her.

And finally relented, his continuing speech grinding out past clenched teeth.

"Deputy Fleming," he said. Stopped. Started again with no less vitriol. "It remains she is here without permission of the Patterson family—"

"She's here investigating a suspicious death," Jill said, still calm and level, almost bored. "She doesn't need permission."

Again Geoffrey seemed to have to work through her rebellion as if unaccustomed to being treated in such an off-hand and disdainful manner. I almost grinned. Almost. But no way was I robbing Jill of her victory. She'd come so far, through so much, become a fantastic cop in the midst of it all and I had her back, knowing she had mine.

Real friends did that sort of thing for one another.

"This is a sensitive day for a young couple who just want to celebrate their nuptials." Oh, he was going to pull out that card, was he? Rub the kid's wedding in my face like that? I bristled while he went on, ignoring me. "Out of respect for them, could we not, at least, remove the cause of family discomfort," this time he did glance my way, flashing me a tight, nasty smile, "until the wedding festivities have ended?"

Jerk. Like Jared and Alicia wanted me gone. Or did they? I did my best not to let his comment influence me. I knew better, right? This was all Marie Patterson's doing. Alicia herself had told me her hands were tied, that the family ran their show, and she wouldn't do anything to put her life with Jared at risk. Fair enough, I guess.

I guess.

My phone buzzed, drawing my attention while I debated fighting Geoffrey on the matter, Jill arching an eyebrow at me as if asking what I'd like to do. Nice to know she was standing there, ready to continue batting for me, when I took note of the name behind the text message and made a choice.

At Petunia's, FBI Special Agent Elizabeth Michaud's message said. *Need to talk ASAP.*

While Geoffrey's attempt to send me scurrying in shame and guilt might have hit a nerve, it wasn't lost on me it was likely Alicia and Jared were, indeed, suffering for my presence. Though, a questionable death in the vicinity should have been more of a downer on their wedding day than having me poking my nose around. Whatever. Crew's ex-partner had the kind of timing that gave me the excuse I needed to leave without losing face.

"I have to take this," I said to Jill, completely ignoring Geoffrey. "Meet you back at the office?"

She nodded to me like that made total sense to her and I spun, stalking off toward the gate, growling under my breath at myself and the realization I, yet again, had a long walk ahead to my car.

Damn it.

I was hot, tired and distinctly cranky by the time I

made it back to Petunia's. It wasn't until I was entering the foyer, I took a second to wonder why Liz was here in the first place. I stood aside to allow two of my guests to exit, managing a smile and a muttered farewell as the pair carried their suitcases out into the September sunshine, waving while the tall, handsome couple waved their enthusiasm back. I slipped into the dim, coolness of the main house entry, tugging the door shut behind me, taking note of the young woman at the sidebar checking yet another pair of people in an endless line of tourists whose faces all blended together.

I hurried past her and into the kitchen, not even trying to greet the girl by name. Not only was I dismally horrid at remembering the personal monikers of my staff—seriously, I had a mental block when it came to faces and names and I had no idea why—we had such a turnover the last year or so it almost seemed fruitless to try, anyway. Though, part of me wondered if the reason our continually revolving employees came and went was because I didn't remember who they were and stumbled through calling them things that had nothing to do with their actual identities.

On the other hand, as I stepped into the kitchen to the scent of dinner cooking and the sight of my mother, her slim form tucked neatly into one of her adorable custom aprons, my pug hunkered at her feet waiting for the inevitable scrap of something to fall to the floor for her to steal, I had to admit it was less me and more the fact that Reading simply was an employee's market. There were so many jobs available that staff had their pick and I doubted very much Petunia's and the annex were unique in the rotating circuit.

I waved at Mom who saluted back with a wooden spoon she'd been using to stir a giant pot of stew in front of her. Liz looked up from where she sat at the kitchen island keeping my mother company, or, more likely, lost in the screen of her phone, smiling one of her rare expressions of happy greeting at me before sipping the coffee Mom likely placed in front of her.

"Fee." Crew's former partner set her mug down, ponytail of darkly shiny hair hanging across the shoulder of her black suit blazer, crisp white shirt looking like she'd ironed it five seconds ago. The slender agent always looked so put together and there had been a time I worried she and Crew had something between them that might keep us apart. But since our engagement, Liz had really seemed to take a liking to me, even coming over a time or two for a beer when our handsome sheriff in common wasn't around, telling me she was making a real effort to get to know me.

It meant a lot and I actually found I rather liked her, too.

"Hey, Liz." I didn't mean to sound grumpy, but it had been a day, you know?

"Sweetheart." Mom's stare wasn't quite accusing, but it was close and I knew her well enough she'd guessed where I'd been. Though, apparently, news of yet another dead person uncovered by yours truly had, as yet, to reach my mother's ears. "Tell me you didn't."

"What?" I sank to the stool next to Liz with a sigh, elbows on the counter, cheeks in my hands as Petunia whined softly and licked her snout in concern. "Go to the wedding?" I shrugged. "Or stumble over a body?"

CHAPTER EIGHT

Mom gaped, the last thing she expected me to say, I guess. She recovered quickly enough while Liz laughed, though she smothered her amusement after a single bark.

"Sorry," the agent muttered. "It's not funny. But seriously." Her dark brown eyes sparkled. "Did you really?"

Grumble. I filled them both in on the case, along with Crew's little act of town defiance making me a deputy. Liz slapped me on the shoulder, grinning, while Mom looked suddenly very worried.

"Welcome to law enforcement, Deputy Fleming," the agent said.

"Fee, you can't possibly accept." Mom hesitated, beautiful face twisting into concern so severe I was about a heartbeat from standing up and hugging her before she pulled herself under control. I'd always thought it was my dad who kept me from being a police officer out of a misplaced—okay, so I was his kid, not so misplaced—need to protect me from the job he loved and that I know was my calling. But I had no idea Mom was so against it, too. How much of her influence led Dad to push my buttons to the point I left Reading and avoided law enforcement altogether?

"It's just a formality," I said, partially to placate my mom and partially to shut Liz down. "The Pattersons weren't happy I snuck onto the property. I think Crew was just trying to keep me from getting arrested for B&E." And, as I said it without thinking, I realized that was exactly what he'd done.

Sigh. I wasn't sure if I should be all gushy over him having my back or pissed off he didn't think I could take care of myself.

"Might come in handy, anyway," Liz said, humor fading. "If what I'm here to talk to you about is true, you could use a badge behind you, Fee."

Mom looked back and forth between us, and I lost the chance to talk to Liz alone when she spoke up. "What are you talking about, Agent Michaud?"

Argh. Just what I needed. Over-protective Mom hovering with a dripping stew spoon giving Petunia enough splatters of tasty yumminess to keep the pug occupied, at least. If only it was so easy to distract my mother.

Liz didn't seem to notice she'd stirred up her own

pot of oh, crap. Instead, she focused on me, frowning, pulling those perfectly arched brows together, bow lips pursed. "Crew hasn't said anything to you about it, has he?"

I gulped. "Is he in trouble?" Please, could we just, for once, catch a break and pretend we might live happily ever after without some kind of disaster crashing our party? I only had three months to go, and I'd be married, at least. Surely, we could make it to Christmas without our lives imploding over something Crew wasn't telling me about his past?

Right, because me finding dead folks and almost dying multiple times wasn't bad enough. Blame it on Crew, Fee. Nice. And yet, he was the one out of town on a mysterious errand he hadn't said a thing about, right? Secrets and death, the ties that bound.

Liz was shaking her head, enough of a denial I knew I was, in fact, the culprit of this particular story. And while I knew Crew was notorious for not filling me in when he thought he was protecting me, my irritation at being kept in the dark simmered a few degrees hotter as Liz spoke.

"I told him to fill you in," she said. "That you deserve to know." Liz shook her head, silken hair shivering in a dark rope of shining threads. I caught the scent of her shampoo while she blew out a soft breath of her own frustration. "He's not doing you any favors keeping you in the dark."

Mom's hand came down on the counter, her expression tight, controlled, demanding. "Spill it." She looked startled then as if her abrupt interruption came as a shock even to her. "If you please, Agent Michaud."

Liz didn't seem put off by my mother's reaction, returning her attention to me. "A profiler friend of mine has been conducting interviews, kind of a pet project of his. He likes to talk to unusual murderers about their crimes." I waited while she sipped her coffee, the last, faint trails of steam rising from the black surface before she went on. "He called me a few days ago, worried. About you. After he interviewed Peggy Malone."

So, the horrible old woman who'd once tried to frame me for her nephew's death and then attempted to murder me, the same woman who'd been my Grandmother Iris's friend, along with Marie Patterson of all people, still lingered in my psyche like a toothache I could never quite shake. Just the sound of her name being spoken made me shiver, took me back to that night in her parlor—now the annex next door—when I'd almost died the first time with her gun pointed at my chest. I glanced down when Petunia moaned softly, a reminder that without the pug that same grandmother left me, I'd likely not be sitting here at the moment.

The dog's shining dark eyes met mine and she snorted once. Did she sense my unease or was it just typical Petunianess that led her to cross to me and sit on my foot while I returned my attention to Liz?

Didn't matter. The feeling of her hot butt on my toes comforted me like nothing else. Except maybe Crew's arms around me. And the chance to give him what for over keeping this from me.

"Peggy holds a massive grudge, Fee," Liz said. "Big enough and scary enough it made my friend pause. And he's been a profiler for two decades." She stared down into her mug. "Said he'd never seen such a level of hate in someone before as he did in her." Her eyes met mine again. "For you." Liz reached out with one hand and grasped mine in a tight grip, her own anxiety finally showing. "Peggy wants you dead, Fee, and if my friend is right, she has a plan to make it happen."

I couldn't respond. What even were words in the wake of such a pronouncement?

Mom, it seemed, didn't have the same inability to be coherent. "But she's in prison." Like that was the be-all and end-all, in her opinion. "For the rest of her life."

Her hopefully short and suffering life, for what my dreams and goals for Peggy Munroe were worth.

"All I know," Liz said, warning in her tone, "is what Harry told me." She paused. "SSA Martingale." I didn't shrug, nod, nada. "According to him, her obsession with you is so consuming, he's concerned she might find a way to reach you despite being incarcerated."

I finally did nod, heavy and hating that even though I'd done my best to put her out of my mind, Peggy's continuing health despite the fact she should never be able to hurt me again, had always lingered as an unhappy reminder my past might catch up with me someday.

"So, since Crew is out of town," Liz went on, brightening, "and considering my insider qualifications to assist, I'll put in for permission to help out with your case. If that's okay with you?"

Wait, what? "Insider qualifications?" I didn't need anyone to look out for me, not even Crew. Where was he again? And why, if I was so independent, thank you very much, did I suddenly feel so much better knowing Liz was going to hang around?

"I might not have been an Olympic hopeful in my day," she said with a wink, "but I know enough about the showjumping world to be of service. Besides, I have time coming and, for some reason I just can't explain, I kind of like it here."

Was she staying for my benefit or my mother's? Because the way Mom sagged into the counter, relief visible on her face, I had my doubts Liz said as much to make me feel better.

"We're delighted to have you, Agent Michaud," Mom said. "If Fee can't make room for you at Petunia's, John and I are happy to have you in our home."

Wow, Mom really was relieved Liz was staying. The agent just shrugged, reaching for her phone again.

"Going to make a call to the office," she said, swinging off her stool like an old-time gunslinger prepping for battle at high noon. "Be right back."

I turned back to Mom when Liz crossed to the kitchen door and spoke quietly into her cell while my mother pretended to smooth the front of her pristine apron, though the bubbling stewpot really needed a stir if she didn't want to burn supper.

"Please, Fee," Mom said then, voice cracking just a little, a glaring sign she was upset as she seemed to realize herself she was neglecting her favorite dinner offering, the long spoon dipping into the rich stew. "Be careful. And take the warning seriously. Peggy Munroe has always been a force to be reckoned with."

Mom didn't have to tell me twice. Though I lingered more so on the fact Crew failed to inform me this problem was even something I needed to obsess over, but, on a lighter note, finding myself grinning at the fact his ex-partner's idea of time off was investigating a murder. And wondering what he'd think of the two of us working together without him here to supervise.

I was usually the source and even I smelled trouble.

CHAPTER NINE

A hasty and rather bossy text message from Olivia Walker interrupted the conversation, probably at the perfect time, though I caught myself scowling at the inordinately snippy tone of the line of letters glaring at me from my cell's glowing screen.

My office. Ten minutes.

Well now. While there were times that text only could be misconstrued and an angle of emotion or intent placed on it that had nothing to do with the sender's actual mental state of the moment, that once known could easily alter the ultimate meaning, it was pretty clear from the mayor's command—no its, buts or ands about it as far as I was concerned—this was obviously not one of those times.

I considered ignoring it. After all, she'd done a

topsy-turvy, backstabbing traitor-to-supporter flip-flop on me that I still wasn't quite willing to let go of and all within the last hour or so. And while not really typical of her—with her own agenda firmly in hand she usually had my back—I expected better from someone who had never found reason to question my loyalty.

Still, as I glared at the phone and thought through the order versus my present mood and whether it was worth it to simply choose to avoid her or not, I sighed over the answer to my silent question. I could take that route, of course, I could. Pretty easy to make that choice, actually. And tempting, the tempting lure of doing my best to pretend I would get my way actually quite delicious.

Except if there was one consistent thing about Olivia Walker, it was her tenacity. I knew I'd only get to enjoy my rebellion from her in a briefly glorious span of time that would end in her showing up, huffing and even more bossy and out of sorts, on my doorstep where she could not only disturb me with her firm and flustered hissy fit, but make a royal pain in her butt of herself for my guests, my business and, worst of all, my mother.

Not that Mom didn't like Olivia, but I'd likely bear the brunt of Lucy Fleming's soft sigh of disappointment I'd let the situation turn into a crap show in my foyer instead of just sucking it up already and doing as I was asked.

Told. Same difference. And though she wasn't standing there with me at that moment, and while I would never expect Mom to tell me to be a pushover, I could hear her clear, calm and reasonable voice as the angel on my shoulder opposed to the devil in me wanting to tell Olivia where she could shove her command. Since Mom would be right and the whole pending mess that really could be easily avoided if I just grit my teeth already won out.

Yeah. My worth it equation when it came to Olivia was based on containing her bossiness to places I could leave her behind, rather than being cornered and looking for a way to force her to leave.

When I told Mom where I was going, glancing curiously at Liz, my mother twisted her lips at me as if fully aware of how irritated I was. I was glad I'd carried out my conversation with her in my own head, rather than in person because now that I saw her reaction I wondered if I'd gauged her own mood right and if she'd have encouraged me to stick it to the mayor rather than told me to be reasonable. Which would have ended badly, I was positive, and with the kind of drama that I really didn't have the strength for right now.

Not that I was attempting to hide my irritation or anything. Bless Mom, she maintained her poise and kept her mouth shut and I chose to believe I'd guessed right in the first place instead of starting the imaginary conversation in real life all over again.

Gah. My brain was so weird.

As for Crew's former partner, she stood, her own phone sliding into her pocket as she buttoned up her blazer and nodded with an air of authority I really had to perfect because it was that badass.

"I'll stop by the sheriff's office," she said, waving to Mom with a small smile and a gesture at the empty mug as way of gratitude for the java. "Text me when you're done with your mayor, and we'll compare notes."

That's how I found myself, still miffed, stomping my way into Olivia's office a few minutes later.

She didn't thank me for coming, circling her desk, the jacket of her pantsuit draped over her chair, thin cream silk shell she wore under it faintly wrinkled from the pressure of the heavier garment she'd set aside. I rarely saw Olivia out of her politician perfect persona but noted the disheveled look of her normally crisp haircut, how the lines around her eyes had deepened, and that there was the faintest tremor in her hand when she waved me into her space before her assistant, Hugh Farcourt, his dark-rimmed glasses barely hiding his concern for her, firmly closed the door behind me.

"Fiona, there you are." Olivia didn't stop to shake my hand or even offer a greeting of any kind, spinning and grasping a file in her grasp before turning back to me. Her lips looked odd, and it wasn't until she spoke again, I realized why. She wasn't wearing lipstick, her normally enhanced mouth now thin and rather lifeless looking without makeup to bring attention to them. I'd been down this road with her before, noted how tired she looked at times, realizing at last she didn't need me to worry about her, that she thrived on stress. And yet, as I did my best to hang onto the last of my annoyance at being summoned in such a fashion, and that I'd actually caved and agreed to the visit, the part of me that felt concern she'd one day push herself too far woke up and paid attention.

"Olivia," I said, taking a step toward her, startled at the level of compassion I felt in a prickling tightness in my chest, "what the hell is going on?"

She didn't answer my question, clutching the file to her, sitting abruptly on the edge of her big, wooden desk, arms clenching the yellow folder against her as if it were the only lifeline she had remaining her. I watched in shock as her left knee jiggled, the heel of her pale pump rising and falling while agitation showed in what looked like an involuntary expression of her present mood.

Instead, she exhaled heavily, glancing over my shoulder at the closed door before meeting my eyes again, her dark ones unreadable. "I have to know," she said, voice low, tight, angry, "despite everything, you have my back."

Um, what? "What's this about?" Now, I could have assured her I did, probably should have. But without the facts, without knowing what this was, exactly, and suspecting the Pattersons had their hands around her throat—one set of hands in particular—there was no way I was giving Olivia any kind of carte blanche, history or not.

She twitched, brows furrowing, deep gashes forming in her forehead and crumpling the makeup she wore into paler lines as she pulled her face into quiet once more.

"You owe me," she said, almost panted, still hugging the file, lower lip trembling.

Nope. Not having this particular conversation. And yet, I guess we were.

"Listen," I snapped, not wanting to be curt or sharp with her but so freaking sick and tired of the lies and half-truths and hidden agendas I'd only seen the edges of for so long I'd finally had it. "For what it's worth, Olivia, we've done each other enough favors along the way I'd like to think saying something like that to me is a hell of a way to get yourself unfriended on social media." She swallowed hard, looked away, while I relented just a bit. "I want to help. I came when you asked, didn't I?" Forget she hadn't asked. I was a big enough woman to give her some credit. "But I need answers and I'm not going to throw myself into the middle of something I don't understand without some kind of information to make my judgment on."

She stared at me, quiet now, and if I was going to be honest with myself, sad. No, I had to be reading her wrong, didn't I? Olivia? Actually showing a genuine emotion that had nothing to do with political motivations? She ran one hand over her face, across her mouth, before she dropped the file on the desk behind her, twisting her torso to do the deed, facing off with me once more, expression now blank, empty and closed off.

"I can see I've misplaced my trust," she said, standing, smoothing the front of her pants with an absent gesture. "How unfortunate."

Wait just a freaking second. I inhaled to argue, more frustrated now than I'd been all day (and that was saying a lot) when her door opened without warning and, of all people, Vivian French walked through.

And in that instant, as I caught the way Olivia's face crumpled at the sight of the Queen of Wheat, how Vivian's relentless icy demeanor triggered that same sorrow I'd seen in the mayor just a moment ago, I had a heartbreaking revelation that had nothing to do with facts, and everything to do with instinct.

I had no idea what happened between the two women, but whatever it was, Vivian won, and Olivia couldn't live with the loss.

But what was the source of the sorrow? I had no idea. Vivian didn't even look at me, gaze focused on the mayor as she spoke.

"We need to talk." She sounded like she was bored. Waited a long moment while Olivia gathered herself, nodded to the bakery owner in the perfect Grace Fiore suit, then to me.

"Thank you, Fiona," Olivia said, voice dull and flat, "that will be all."

I could have pushed the issue and thought about it for a long breath. Something truly horrible was about to happen, I could feel it. But as I considered holding my ground, demanding answers, Vivian's head turned, just barely, her jaw tightening, gaze flickering to the side, pale eyes resting on me.

She didn't move otherwise, didn't ask me to go. She didn't have to. I felt her compel me to just leave already and, despite myself, I did as she wanted, spinning and stalking out of the office, grumbling under my breath, telling myself I was leaving because this was clearly a waste of time and not because Vivian French wanted me to.

Knowing I was lying to myself.

As particularly unsatisfying as that conversation had been, I had a suspicious death to investigate thanks to my over-protective fiancé.

Funny, usually my busybody desire to dig into murder I was supposed to stay out of was the reason I felt frustrated. Now that I'd been offered the chance to do so legitimately? I had bigger issues I wished I could make my priority.

I really needed to make up my mind already.

CHAPTER TEN

I texted Liz, but not before Jill's message came through when I set foot on the sidewalk outside town hall.

Head back to the center, the deputy sent. *Could use the backup.*

Liz get in touch? I climbed into the front seat of my car as Jill responded.

Yup, she sent. *Bring her.*

Okay then. A quick drive down the block carried me to the steps to the sheriff's office where Liz stood waiting, her dark sunglasses making her look even more the special agent. She waved while she descended the stairs, climbing into the passenger's seat without a word. Nope, those she saved for after I pulled away, taking a right at the stop sign on the corner, heading out to the edge of town and the drive up the mountain while she spoke.

"That cousin of yours," she said, so droll I glanced sideways with a start, the tight line of her normally full lips making me grimace. "He's quite the character."

She was clearly holding back. Hopefully not for my benefit. Surely Crew had told her there was no love lost between me and Robert. "Had a bit of a conversation with the waste of space and clean oxygen, did you?"

Liz grinned suddenly, though there was little joy in it, her eyes hidden behind the aviators across her gaze though I could guess I'd see annoyance there.

"He's still questioning Sarah Shard," she said. "Been at it for two hours. The girl is exhausted." A little quiver of worry for Pamela's niece did a dance through my tummy while Liz stared out the passenger window, right arm resting on the door. "Useless, but at least he's distracted. According to Turner, that's a good thing?" Her head turned, dark lenses focused on me, that last what should be a statement rising in tone at the end into a question.

So, they had discussed Reading. Likely at length. Which made me wonder how much he'd told her about me. Not that it mattered at the moment. Seriously, was I making this about Fiona Fleming? Naturally. Despite the fact Liz clearly made the choice to like me and include me, I still caught myself worrying in faint anxiety what she thought of me.

Silly. Grow up, kid.

"Definitely a good thing." I felt the urge to fall into whiny complaint about Robert bite at the edges of my mood and chose otherwise. Surely someone as professional as Liz didn't want to spend the fifteen-minute drive to the center listening to me natter on about my vile cousin. Instead, I filled her in on what I knew of the case while she listened silently, still as stone. She nodded a few times, her head turning just a bit as she seemed to identify the moment I edited out why I was in the stable—my excuse I ducked in to avoid security didn't pass her scrutiny and nor should it have, considering how long she'd been picking out people's lies and omissions thanks to her job—but she didn't ask any questions so I hurried on, hating that I felt guilty for not telling her all the truth.

I comforted myself in the fact I intended to tell Crew just as soon as he got back. Because he needed to know. As for Liz, I was sure what happened to Melina Canty had nothing at all to do with the mysterious conversation between Robert and who I was positive was Marie Patterson.

Okay, at least 99% sure.

When we pulled into the parking lot at the center, my little sedan settling beside Jill's cruiser, Liz paused while I unbuckled my seat belt and tossed my keys into the open mouth of my big purse. I waited as she seemed to absorb what I'd told her, about the fight I'd witnessed—both of them, if the one between Melina and Gretchen with Charlie watching had significance—about Sarah's clear animosity toward the dead woman, Violet's horrible demeanor, Jimmy's apparent attraction to the young woman in custody, and the aggravated conversation between Melina and Alphonse Brunbaugh.

She slowly unhooked her own belt before turning to me, sliding her glasses off so her dark brown eyes met mine, level and steady an instant before she laughed. Out loud. Startling me so much I grinned back.

"I knew about you, of course," she said. "Turner told me a lot, especially at first. How you just kind of," she raised her eyebrows at me, wiggling them, "fall into trouble. Seem to be at the wrong place at the right time. Or is that the right place at the wrong time?" She snorted. "Body magnet, he calls you." Lovely. Wasn't sure that was the term of endearment I'd been hoping for from the man I was marrying. "Well, used to," she corrected herself, though it didn't seem to be out of need to soothe my feelings, so I accepted her altered comment and forgave Crew who, technically, didn't need to be forgiven because he was right, wasn't he? "Either you have the worst freaking luck of anyone I've ever encountered," Liz finished, winking, "or you're made for this job, Fee." She pushed her glasses back into place, the faint scent of whatever she used to wash her hair or her clothes wafting toward me as her suitcoat rustled, the open jacket exposing the gun at her waist a moment before she opened the door. "I'm going to guess both."

I followed her out of the car, wishing she was

wrong, knowing she was likely right. I was exactly where I was supposed to be, doing exactly what I was meant to be doing and, as I crossed to the main gate at Liz's side, noting she paused her step enough so we could walk in stride instead of pushing on ahead of me like I expected her to (another reason to really, really like and respect her) I realized the actual reason I'd never felt exactly fulfilled in New York. Or anywhere outside Reading.

Home was where the murder was.

Jill was waiting for us, her own sunglasses casting mirrored reflections of us, a soft tip of the brim of her deputy's hat greeted by a similar and almost universal nod of recognition from Liz that screamed law enforcement solidarity. As for me, the little wave I offered the deputy felt like I was doing my best to fit in with the cool kids and only managed to make it to awkward but neither of the women seemed to care.

Bless them. I suddenly felt less like an outsider and actually like this might be fun. Right, because someone else's death was fun, Fee.

Jill handed me a badge with a grin, though when I raised my eyebrows at her as I took it, she shook her head with a soft laugh.

"You have to qualify for a gun," she said.

Well, crappy. But all good. "Thanks, Jill."

She slipped a sheet of paper out of the inside pocket of her dark green jacket, Liz helping herself while the deputy went on. "Judge Grant was kind enough to give us a court order allowing you on the property for the course of the investigation," she said. "Pattersons be damned." As far as I knew the founding family had everyone in town aside from those closest to me in their pocketbooks. How had Jill managed it? "Hugh just delivered it." Ah, so she hadn't. Jill seemed a bit perplexed by the personal delivery of the paperwork from Olivia's assistant, and I agreed with her. The mayor had made sure I had what I needed to pretend I was a real police officer? Even after she'd seemed to write me off as a supporter?

What was Olivia really up to?

That question would have to wait. Liz handed the page back to Jill, hands tucking back her jacket, fingers splayed on her waist as she cocked one hip and addressed us both. "Thanks for letting me in on this, deputy." Jill's startled smile and nod told me she wasn't expecting that kind of respect from the agent, though I wasn't surprised by it, not now. Still, raising estimations of herself? Check. "I know Crew asked you to, but it means a lot having your support."

"My pleasure," Jill murmured. "You'll be taking lead, Agent Michaud?"

Liz shook her head, silken ponytail swinging as she looked away, lips pursed. "Crew speaks highly of your talents," she said. "I'm happy to follow you, Wagner. Besides, I'm a newcomer here. Might be prudent to have you continue as lead with the two of us backing you up."

Jill's chest swelled just a bit. "Roger that."

I'd been witness to male egos, both bolstering

and knocking each other down, but I'd never witnessed this kind of powerful women in law enforcement booster club show before. It almost made me emotional.

My phone rang, interrupting, and I turned aside while the amazing women I admired even more now bent their heads and let me have a private moment with my fiancé.

"Sweetheart," he said, sounding tired. "Are you okay?"

"I'm fine," I said, suddenly worried. Why was he tired? Where had he gone? His assurance when I dropped him at the airport that he was out of town a day or two was an easy sell when I was sucked into wedding bitterness. Not like me at all to resist demanding specifics. While he'd kept secrets from me in the past, I'd thought such a need to hide what he was doing was long gone. Mind you, I hadn't pushed, but the tone of his voice, the way he sounded anxious but distracted, told me whatever he was up to, it was time to find out what he was keeping from me.

I was patient, but only to a point. Okay, stop laughing.

"I'm sorry I wasn't there for you." His distress grew, the chatter of people in the background of wherever he'd found himself loud enough I made out a few voices I didn't recognize. "Especially today of all days." The wedding, yeah. "I hope you know I had no choice."

"Are you going to tell me what's going on?" I did

my best to keep my tone level and quiet, squashing any judgments or leaps to conclusions that might upset him. Because he really sounded like he was wrung out. And I was doing my best to learn to put him on my priority list for understanding and benefit of the doubt, so I didn't end up divorced shortly after we got married. Nice of me, right?

He hesitated then sighed. "It's personal, old family stuff. I'll tell you everything when I get back." I wanted to ask for more and bit my tongue. He said he'd tell me. And I knew perfectly well despite the fact he loved me he still struggled with the loss of Michelle, his former wife. Did this have something to do with her death? It had happened years ago, so surely not. "I'm in California," he said then, confirming he was a lot further away than he'd led me to believe. "I'm sorry I didn't tell you but when I got the call, I left without thinking." So, I wasn't the only one who had to learn to make the other a priority. Fair enough. That actually made me feel better. "I keep forgetting I'm not alone anymore."

Okay, so that last statement? Spoken with a soft hitch at the end like he was fighting tears? Triggered mine and made me choke up, forgive him anything, want to reach through the cell phone and hug him so hard.

"You do what you have to," I said, firm and loving and warm, "and I'll be here when you're done. I love you, Crew. Whatever it is, whatever you need, I'm here."

It took him a long time to respond, and his voice

still shook with emotion when he finally did. "I love you too, Fee. I'm grateful every day for you. For us." He swallowed audibly, coughed softly to clear what had to be tension in his own throat while I clutched the phone tightly to my ear, other hand covering my heart because it was all I had at the moment.

"I'm going to be a bit longer than I thought," he said then. "A few more days. Liz is with you?" Hope in that question.

"She's with Jill right now," I said, turning back to find the two watching me, though they kept their distance and neither looked impatient. "We're digging into the case now." I crossed to them, lowering the phone and tapping the small icon that would broadcast his voice. "You're on speaker, Crew."

"Hey, Turner," Liz spoke up first. "Just like you to slack off when there's a murder to solve." Her tone didn't match her words and from the faint sorrow in her voice, I knew she knew exactly where he was and why. Chest clench. I forced the instinctual reaction to release as Crew spoke.

"Don't get comfortable, Michaud," he said. "Jill, you and Fee make sure she's made most unwelcome, you hear?" He was forcing joviality, but it worked, Liz grinning, Jill snorting a laugh.

"Yes, sir," she said. "We've got it handled."

"I just bet." He sighed. "Tread lightly, but don't hesitate to dig if you're being stonewalled. The Pattersons might think they own Reading, but the victim deserves justice."

"I'll call you later," I said. "Okay?"

"I'm on a three-hour time difference," he said. "Tonight?" I didn't get to respond. "Good luck with the case. Fee, can I talk to you privately again, please?" I took him off speaker, eyes locked on Liz as he spoke again. "Tell Michaud about the treasure, Fee."

Um, what? Before I could ask him why he thought that was such a good idea, someone spoke to him, the interruption muffled but audible.

"I have to go, sweetheart," he said. "I love you. Be safe." He hesitated before sighing. "Please, be careful." And then, he was gone.

CHAPTER ELEVEN

"I'm sorry, Miss Fleming," Gretchen Latrell said, turning her back on me. "I can't talk to you."

"Deputy," I growled between clenched teeth, doing my best not to let my redheaded temper out into the light while it begged me for freedom. "*Deputy* Fleming."

The facility manager shrugged, circling her desk and heading for her chair, her small but well-appointed office cluttered with files, riding gear and heavy with the scent of saddle soap and horses. "*Doctor*," she said, stressing her own title. Now, I had, admittedly, addressed her as Ms. Latrell, so my bad. Still. Want to firmly annoy me and ensure we're never going to be friends? Throw my mistake back in my face and treat me like I'm intruding when I'm only doing my job.

Growl.

"Regardless of your employment status," she said, crisp, official, her broad shoulders shrugging as she sank her tall, muscular body into the leather seat, hands folding across her stomach while she rested her elbows on the armrests, "I'll wait for Deputy Wagner or Agent Michaud." Said in a tone that screamed she didn't believe I was a real police officer so why should she bother? And her cycle of making me her enemy for life continued. "Was there anything else?"

There was. A whole heaping pile of other things I wanted to say, scream, throw around the room while I had an epic temper tantrum and let out all of the frustration that had been building the last hour, I'd managed to receive this self-same response from every single person I'd attempted to question.

Every. Single. One.

Because despite her attitude and attempt to make me go ballistic over something she couldn't have known was giving me a serious case of the frauds (yes, carrying the badge left a queasy feeling in my stomach along with a deeply penetrating knowing I shouldn't be here, asking her questions, pretending to be a cop when it was all a show to keep me from getting arrested for B&E), I guess I shouldn't have been surprised to be held behind a solid wall of hell no, though, right? After all, when I'd passed through the gates with Liz and Jill, sighing over the fact there was a wedding celebration going on not so far away—and maybe I could sneak off now that I had permission just to get a glimpse because that wasn't a conflict of interest or anything, right? —I was almost immediately stonewalled.

First person to do so? Geoffrey Jenkins, standing with his arms crossed over his chest, those two hired guns at his side hulking their threatening personages behind him, just inside the main gate.

Jill immediately presented the court order which Geoffrey took his good old time reviewing before handing it back to the deputy with a smug look on his face.

"We will, of course, follow the letter of the law," he said. "Miss Fleming—"

"Deputy Fleming," I said, half of me liking the sound of that, the other (more reasonable and logical) part of me internally cringing at the fact I had the audacity to play this role at all.

"—may investigate this crime. However, she is to be restricted to this immediate area." He gestured around himself like he expected me to stand in one tiny spot and not move a muscle.

Right, that was going to happen. Silenced my inner critic, sure did. Because he clearly understood what investigating a murder required. As in, moving around? Poking my nose into places previously unwelcome? And likely still unwelcome, but too bad, so sad, not in the mood for games right now.

And carrying a damned badge, so snap.

Jill's scowl told me she was on board with my line of thought—the line that wanted me to be a cop, thanks. The reasonable voice who thought I should just go home and be grateful I wasn't in a cell with the Pattersons pressing charges? She could suck it. "The court order states *Deputy* Fleming," nice of her to stress the title like that, girl had my *back*, "is permitted access to the facility, Mr. Jenkins." Wow. Jill called me deputy. She thought I was authentic, had to. Jill would be the first one to ask me to please be reasonable if she didn't think I should be here. Right?

Sure, Fee. Keep telling yourself the stories you need to hear in order to not pursue the art of minding your own business.

"And she has access," he said. "To *this* spot."

Was he freaking kidding me?

Liz's turn, apparently. She slowly removed her sunglasses, all super smooth special agent that made me shiver with holy crap how awesome was she while she tucked back the front of her jacket so Geoffrey could see her gun, her badge. She didn't hurry, slipping her sunnies into her interior blazer pocket, seemingly taking her time getting them squared away before she spoke in the coolest, calmest voice ever.

"Letter of the law or not," she said, "Deputy Fleming is on this case, Mr. Jenkins." Shiver. FBI Special Agent Elizabeth Michaud called me deputy, too. Did that make it official? Could the internal fraud police stand down? "Now, step aside or I'll arrest you for obstruction."

The two black-clad bullies flexed. I saw them do

it, at exactly the same time. As if to threaten the small, stunning agent with their bulky muscles and big guns strapped to their tree-trunk thighs, their impressive heights and broad shoulders making me a bit nervous and think about maybe going home after all, now that I considered things carefully, no harm, no foul.

Liz? Yeah, she'd clearly dealt with their type before. Instead of saying a thing, she stood there, still Miss Casual Freaking Superhero FBI agent, one eyebrow cocked, looking back and forth between the hired guns a long moment before—I kid you not—they both backed down.

Oh my *god*. If Crew backed out of our relationship for some insane reason, I was going to marry *her*. Or at least make her teach me how the hell she did that. Because, whoa.

Who me, go home? After that show of confident support that should win her an Oscar and a Nobel Peace Prize and status as Queen of the World who owned their collective security grunt butts?

Never. I'd rather die than let that awesome show of woman power go to waste.

Liz returned her attention to Geoffrey who looked suddenly less confident. Man had a brain, I'd give him that. "Now, if you would please allow us to do our job," she said. "I'm sure we'll have this whole sad affair wrapped up in short order." She turned to Jill, to me, and nodded. "Officers. Shall we?" She didn't wait to find out if Geoffrey was going to protest if his security bullies would argue. Instead, she spun and strode off, as if expecting the entire world to deliver to her exactly what she asked for, right now, no waiting, hell yeah.

I needed more Liz in my life.

We split up at that point, Jill staying behind to talk to Geoffrey and ask him questions. I heard her mention the guest list and knew the Pattersons would be suitably distracted by her request, hopefully enough to give Liz and me the time we needed to investigate before they found another way to interfere.

Liz slowed as I hurried after her, enough that it felt like she hadn't done it on purpose, that we'd meant for this to unfold the way it had, and I resisted the urge to hug her for her amazingness.

"Let's split up the suspects," she said, "tackle more in less time." She glanced over her shoulder, still at ease but tension in her voice. "I know that type, Fee. He's going to get in the way again. So, if we can do as much as possible now, it'll save us arguments later." She wasn't as inwardly confident as she seemed on the outside? Gave me hope I could actually maybe master that cool awesome she walked around in. Though it also made me wonder if I was overestimating what she could accomplish.

Forget that. She was a hero in my books.

"Funny," she said as we divvied up the list and prepared to head our separate ways. She glanced one more time at Geoffrey and the black-clad boys who stared at us like we were prey, target practice. "Why ever would a wedding require that kind of firepower?"

I didn't comment, had a twinge of guilt yet again about not telling her everything, especially in light of the fact Crew wanted me to fill her in on the treasure. And that I now trusted her completely, as I knew he did. But informing her about the Pattersons, about my suspicions that had zero real proof or merit, all rumor, innuendo, speculation and personal anecdotes, would take far too long and was better delivered over a cold beer with our feet up rather than in the middle of a suspicious death investigation.

So, later then. And we'd see if telling Liz everything got me new insights or more problems.

Speaking of problems, my first appeared almost immediately after I knocked on Violet Perry's door and tried to ask her questions. She clammed up, slammed the door in my face and forced me to pound on it and make a general insistent pain in the rear end of myself before she'd open it again.

When she did, the snarky little creature tossed her hair, now down around her shoulders, her tiny body sheathed in the most current and expensive yoga gear known to woman.

"I don't have to talk to a fake cop," she said. "Send a real one." And, with that, she slammed the door once more while I fumed on the other side and considered my options.

I could freak out, lose my temper, knock down her door and kick her butt. I could walk away, go question someone else. Or I could go home.

Yeah. Temper, temper. And not leaving. Guess which one I picked?

Except, as I did my best to circulate through the four names Liz assigned me, Jimmy Hogan and Alphonse Brunbaugh among them, I was met with more refusal, flat out disdain and in the case of Gretchen, understanding of the real reason I was being stonewalled.

The Pattersons. Clearly, Geoffrey had spoken to them first, informing them to keep quiet and not tell me a thing. So, I might have won the battle with Olivia's little court order, and the struggle with Liz at my side, her FBI presence enough to get me past the gatekeepers, but I was on my own when it came to cajoling uncooperative suspects.

CHAPTER TWELVE

I stormed out of Gretchen's office, furious, feeling impotent and as if I'd been assaulted, my stomach in knots. Typically, I could get people to talk to me, usually getting them to spill far more than they originally intended. This clamming up, walling off, tight-lipped action? Wasn't used to it, not even a little bit. I realized then, as I stalked toward the stable that hosted the crime scene, sun already set behind the mountains and real night rapidly approaching, this was how real cops usually felt and half-stumbled a step before catching myself in that truth. Up to now, I had the benefit of being an innocuous and non-threatening presence when I was "just" a bed and breakfast owner. Everyone I spoke to, all the suspects and hangers-on and people I'd connected to the cases I'd poked my nose in didn't see a badge when they'd overshared. They'd seen a redhead in a ponytail and a dirty t-shirt with dishpan hands and an earnest, innocent expression they'd handed their info over to.

Okay, so I was imagining that was who they saw. Still, without this star I now wore on my hip, attached to my belt (because that was where the cool kids wore it, right?) I held no authority and, subsequently, zero intimidation factor. Now that I was a deputy? The Pattersons and their roadblocks aside, I was finally experiencing what being an officer of the law was really like.

And it sucked, quite frankly. A *lot*. Gave me a huge insight into the officers I knew. My dad, Jill, Liz, Crew. Even (gross) Robert. Did Jill's boyfriend, Ranger Matt Winston, also experience this kind of closed-mouthed reaction from people? And was this only something they met up with when a major crime investigation was underway or were they treated like this all the time by those who didn't know them but were privy to the fact they upheld the law as a profession?

It was almost enough to make me biff the badge Crew had kindly granted me into the distant grass and head for home. Except, of course, I didn't. Because I wouldn't dishonor them or this profession by quitting so easily. While he'd likely chosen to make me a deputy to protect me, Crew knew I'd take the role seriously. That I'd be digging into the death on my own regardless. He hadn't made this choice to lend me his authority—and that of the town—lightly. I knew my fiancé better than that. Not to mention the fact Liz had gone to bat for me with Geoffrey, as had Jill. And Dad always had my back.

Abandoning this job because it was hard? Nope. Not Fiona Fleming.

But I did realize I had to go about things a different way this time around or end up going mental while yelling at everyone around me in sheer frustration. I paused at the rear entrance to the stable, glaring at the dumpster now lit by a large, bright light shining from the peak of the building, illumination likely triggered by the loss of sunlight, and had a thought. Well, if no one would talk to me, maybe there was some physical evidence I could uncover. I hadn't expected to be on refuse duty, but it wasn't like I hadn't been elbow deep in garbage before. Running Petunia's meant handling all kinds of messes, didn't it?

Okay then. It was a dirty job, and I was going to do it.

I returned to Jill and retrieved a pair of gloves from her while she continued her conversation with Geoffrey. Apparently, they'd been at it since I left with Liz a half-hour before. Bless my friend's huge and noble heart, from the pink in her cheeks and the snap in her eyes, even Jill's epic patience and professionalism were wearing thin. I hurried off, feeling like a coward, leaving her to deal with him and the Patterson version of let's be jerkfaces and impede an investigation to the utmost of our ability.

She was lead, though. Her job. Still. I owed her.

I focused on the dumpster, ignoring the looks from a pair of riders who walked past like I was invading their privacy. You know what? They could suck it. The big metal lid reverberated as it slammed open and I was grateful I'd been continuing my runs and workouts with Crew when I hopped up to the lip and swung myself inside, gloves in place. Sure, as I landed on my sneakered feet in the refuse of the stable, I had to wonder at my gratitude. Yes, I was in the best shape of my life thanks to my fiancé and our penchant for using some of our time together to exercise. But in the face of a pile of garbage (I really should have been wearing a full suit and booties and decided to ask forgiveness later if the forensics got messed up), I found myself scowling instead.

The likelihood there was anything in the trash of help was the only thing keeping me from feeling too guilty about not following technical procedure. I just needed something to do. I shuffled my feet, poking about a bit, dejected by the end of my feeble search. I uncovered a box of dark hair dye, the remnants of the included gloves and the bottle of the leftovers making me sigh. Great, so some of the riders colored their hair. Huge evidence, absolutely vital when someone died.

Way to go, Fee.

I heaved my way out and onto the ground again, closing the lid of the dumpster, catching sight of the manure pile not so far away. And sighed in defeat. Fine. If I was going to dig through garbage? I could lower my standards all the way to the gutter and rifle through a pile of horse dung.

Because that was where my talents had been relegated, thanks to the Pattersons.

I was on my way to said heap of equine refuse when I spotted Charlie Chaswick pushing an overloaded wheelbarrow, exiting one of the other stables. I hurried toward him despite knowing he wasn't on my list, that Liz could have gotten to him already. The hope I could get someone, anyone, to talk to me, even if they'd already been interrogated, stirred up my blood and returned my optimism.

Yeah, shouldn't have gotten my hopes up. Charlie took one startled look at me, dumped his load, and spun, practically running back toward the stable with his wheelbarrow rattling over the ground, the big, rubber tire bouncing when he hit a small pothole before disappearing inside the dimness of the building.

Snarl. He didn't deserve to be the brunt of my irritation, but for all I knew he was responsible for Melina's death, right? So, he could take a bit of Fleming frustration and be grateful I didn't unleash the full brunt of my temper.

Yet.

I entered the stable at a huffing walk, heard the sound of a pitchfork scraping on concrete, spotted the flying mass of used straw heading for the barrow and cornered Charlie inside the stall. He swallowed, looking over my shoulder, shaking his head before I could say a word.

"Please, ma'am," he said, "I'll get fired if I talk to you. And I really need this job."

Argh. I could have lingered, pressed him, but he looked nervous enough and innocent to boot, so I shot him a glare instead and left, kicking at the little piles of fallen straw and dung he'd dropped in one of his trips to the main pile.

I found myself standing in front of it, scowling, gloved hands in my pockets, the kind of anger I usually reserved for people who'd wronged me aimed at that mass of horse droppings and used bedding. The gathering dark cast shadows from the pile, in heavy contrast with the bright light overhead, making everything seem eerie and rather sharply focused. At least Charlie had confirmed what I already knew in my heart. He'd been told to stay quiet, to not talk to me. And that meant, at the very least, the Pattersons were, in fact, interfering with the investigation. I perked just a bit. I could tell Jill and Liz as much. Maybe there was good that could come out of this. If they continued to purposefully get in the way of law enforcement, perhaps we could use that to force our way into the Patterson family's secrets...?

I was stalling. And lying to myself. Because despite the fact I was used to messes, this giant, steaming pile of poop reacting to the cooling temperature as night fell? Seemed to represent exactly my life's path at this exact moment. Yes, I was marrying the man of my dreams. Yes, my businesses were busy and thriving. But the stinking underbelly of my town? The secrets and darkness and all the lies I had, as yet, to uncover? Lurked like this manure behind the pretty facade of Reading, Vermont.

The cutest town in America needed its crap turned over so it could air itself out.

I wasn't proud of my temper, or the expression of it that made me lash out with one sneaker, kicking at a clump of manure, sending it flying. But it did deliver the kind of startling result that, in the end, made my show of anger worth it.

Something shiny and small flew from the toe of my runners and impacted the side of the stable, ringing softly as it struck. All angst forgotten, I circled the pile and approached where the item landed, crouching to examine it, cell phone snapping a picture—never mind the original resting place had been compromised, no one needed to know that, right? —of the big syringe, the needle's tip catching the light, slightly bent from, I guessed, impact with the building, lying in a small clump of grass.

I picked it up after taking several shots, wrapping it inside the glove I slipped from my hand and around the item, using the other to secure it completely. No, I might not have been successful in interrogating suspects, but maybe I'd found a clue.

Regardless, it was apparent I was useless here and finally admitted it to myself. I stood with a sigh and texted Liz a quick message to that effect before heading to the gate and Jill with my prize.

CHAPTER THIRTEEN

Geoffrey was just driving off in his ridiculous car, his two security boys lurking at the entrance when I rejoined Jill. She didn't say anything about the long and clearly arduous conversation she'd endured, but from the curt way she waved off my evidence she was struggling to maintain her composure.

"Just take it to the doc," she grumbled before marching off. To where? Only Jill knew.

Got it. Doing my job and staying out of her way.

I took a moment to reinforce Liz's power move and waved cheerily at the black-clad mercenary on my left when I walked out, the best I could do and about one step back from flashing him a very rude gesture that involved my middle finger. Would likely have undermined what the FBI agent had done for me. Besides, it was much more satisfying to be happy in the face of his scowling than angry and generated the furious flash of frustration I was hoping for.

Nice to know someone else was suffering along with me.

At least, I told myself he was suffering as I drove across town, toward the highway and the hospital Dr. Aberstock called home. Sorry, work. Which amounted to home for me, so the correlation between the two came naturally.

I parked in the lot at the back of the large, white building, avoiding a pair of EMTs who hurried out the emergency doors and into their white and orange zigzag painted ambulance before racing off again, skirting a pair of families who made their way, one with smiles, the other weighed down by sorrow, toward the ER entrance. I didn't have time for their stories, the small regional hospital caring for people outside Reading which meant I didn't recognize anyone I met on my way to the plain, innocuous entry to the morgue.

I entered without hesitation since I'd been here before, the heavy scent of disinfectant and lingering death catching at the back of my throat. My sneakers squeaked on the shiny vinyl floor, quiet hallway devoid of sound but the humming fluorescents overhead. Weird, it felt different being here this time. Was it the badge on my belt? Or the fact I was alone instead of in Crew's company? I felt official and, for the first time since I'd been handed the star that made me a member of the Reading Sheriff's

Department like I actually might be important to the case. Valuable. Necessary, even. Jill had trusted me with this task, right? Sure, the clue I found might not have been relevant, but I was providing a thoughtful and professional presence to the case.

Like a real cop. And that put a bit of a spring in my step and a surge of confidence in my heart that carried me to the end of the hall without a moment's doubt.

That ended abruptly when I realized the man I'd come to see wasn't present at the moment. Instead, as I firmly pushed my way through the large swinging door and into the main room of the morgue, I stopped in my tracks at the sight of Barry Clement, Dr. Aberstock's assistant/lurker/creepy-crawly who, despite an early positive assessment by yours truly, had rapidly devolved into the kind of cowardly lowlife I despised on sight.

We'd avoided each other as best we could because, from the sour look on Barry's face, the feeling was mutual. Fair enough. I didn't need him to like me, after all. When he inhaled to protest me being there—oh, I could see it on his face he wanted to protest—I had a flare of doubt that died when I seized on, of all people, Mom and her amazing confidence. It was her in my head, my incredible mother's steadiness, that moved my hand down to my waist, unclipping the sign of my new status, and flashed the badge Jill gave me with something akin to a challenge.

Tinged with the edges of hysterical amusement.

He gaped like I'd slapped him. Made it all worth it. Petty, who, me? Maybe not worthy of Mom's silent presence or the fact I'd used what I'd learned from her to get this far, but… well.

Guilty, your honor.

And take that, you smarmy little weasel.

"I have evidence that might be relevant in the Melinda Canty murder." Okay, again, I was reaching. For all I knew this syringe had been used to doctor a horse. But the fact it wasn't disposed of properly gave me enough impetus to make my claim. I held out the glove-wrapped syringe while Barry shook his head, hands tucked behind his back.

"I'm not taking possession," he said, "not from—" He paused, frowned again. "There are proper channels, you know."

It wasn't lost on me he meant to say, "Not from you," and that he was covering his tracks. So, the Pattersons were behind his lack of enthusiasm, were they? I could only guess that was the case and had been kind of leaning in that direction of belief for a while now. Didn't make me any less angry, though.

"What is your problem, anyway?" It had been a long day, begun by hopping a fence, getting tangled in an argument that wasn't mine, being escorted out like a criminal, hopping the fence again, sneaking around like a thief, overhearing a conversation that left me with more questions than answers, stumbling over an(other) dead body, missing my friend's wedding, being made a deputy, having a new friend arrested, all capped off by this ridiculous and acutely irritating attempt everyone connected to Marie Patterson seemed to have to tweak my very last nerve.

Barry's face compacted into obvious dislike, something he'd never actually shared with me before. It only lasted a moment but was long enough I lost the last shred of giving a crap about him or what happened to him as he spoke.

"Maybe if you would learn your place," he snapped as if he'd finally had it himself. "Stop digging into things that don't concern you." Wow, he sounded like Robert. And the old Crew. "You're only going to bring more trouble to Reading, you know, if you don't mind your own business."

What was that supposed to mean? "What kind of trouble?"

Barry swallowed, wiping at his mouth with one hand, the front of his lab coat crumpled where his other set of fingers twisted the fabric into a knot he didn't seem to notice he was making.

"Just, lay off already," he said. "There are others in this town trying to get through life. We don't need you making a mess of everything."

Grunt. I closed the distance between us, knowing it might be misconstrued as threatening but wanting to get in his face a little. "Are you implying I'm causing you grief, Barry?" Okay, so I may have been feeling a little guilty after all. Just a little. Like, minuscule. But yeah.

Guilty.

"You're making trouble for everyone," he

snapped, finishing what I started, in my space. "The mayor, your precious sheriff. Dr. Aberstock included." I blinked as he went on—

The dock rocked under my feet, Vivian's piercing screams making my head ache, Victor sinking, sinking while the shadow paused one last moment before fleeing—

Whoa. That again? What gave? Barry didn't recognize I'd flashed back, clearly, but my silence seemed to give him courage. His volume rose, a faint sheen of sweat on his upper lip and broad forehead as he shook ever so slightly, carrying on while I struggled to pull myself fully back to the present. "You think you're all that, Fiona Fleming. But you don't care about what happens to anyone as long as you get what you want."

"Which is?" I startled myself with my calm and compassion. I hadn't been expecting this conversation and, from my reaction, Barry hadn't been, either. Usually, I would have lost my temper in the face of such a challenge from someone I really didn't like. But he'd triggered my doubts about myself, and since he was clearly and honestly upset, there had to be something to it. Right?

Besides, the flashbacks I was living through were shaking me to the core and I found it hard to muster anger when I had the recurring death of Victor French lurking in the back of my mind, the truth of his demise unanswered.

So I waited and held my temper and let him talk. Go me.

But he didn't get to go on. The door swung and

Dr. Aberstock hustled in, huffing as he almost ran into me. He took one look between me and Barry and the kindly old Santa Claus clone took on a distinctly unhappy expression that had nothing to do with my presence.

At least, if the glare he shot at his assistant followed by a jabbing index finger was any indication. "Mr. Clement," Dr. Aberstock snapped before flicking said finger at the exit. "Out!"

Barry's childish reaction of sullen retreat dashed my feelings of guilt. Dr. Aberstock waited until the young man had left before his own expression relented, a small smile of welcome on his face. He glanced down at the glove-wrapped present in my hand and chuckled then, waving me inside.

"Brought me a treat, did you?" He set his doctor's case on the stainless steel table (yes, he still carried one of those bowling ball bags around, imagine, stuffed with a stethoscope and gloves of his own along with assorted medical paraphernalia, not to mention the sucker collection I'd been privy to thanks to the many times he'd had to check me over) and turned toward me, fishing out a pair of gloves from the box on the rolling stand next to it. I deposited the syringe in his grasp and watched him unfold the prize, frowning as he did, but in curiosity, not upset.

Whatever was going on between Dr. Aberstock and Barry, he didn't comment on it or my presence, though he did waggle his eyebrows at the badge in my hand.

"Crew's made an honest woman of you, I see." He grinned openly, chuckling again. "I made a funny."

I laughed too. Sure, this town might have those who wanted me out of the way, but I still had my friends and those who supported me. And the kindly older doctor had always been one of the latter, if not the former, to boot. Wait, he'd been at the crime scene, gathered the body personally, dressed in his usual jeans and button-up. All indicators he hadn't been interrupted at the wedding for surely, he would have been in a suit if he'd been on the guest list? I might have been reading too much into it. Perhaps he was on call. Or did the good doctor decide to decline an invitation—or miss out on one altogether?

Was that part of the trouble I'd brought to Dr. Aberstock according to Barry?

"Doc," I said, "if Barry's giving you grief…" I didn't finish the obvious question: why not just fire his ass?

The doctor shrugged, calculated grin tight and mysterious. "There's an old saying about enemies and friends, my dear Fiona," he said. "And there are times knowing there's a fox in the henhouse is much more valuable than not knowing where the eggs are going."

The clever old reprobate. "You're far too smart for your own good," I said.

He winked. "That makes two of us." He didn't seem particularly stressed about it, back to his normal good-natured banter, so I did something I rarely did.

I backed off. Dr. Aberstock clearly had his situation sorted and, not that I was taking what Barry said to heart, but… if me poking my nose in was making trouble for the kindly doctor, I needed to just let him handle his wheelhouse.

So there. I *could* mind my own business.

I thought about asking him more about the death of Victor French. Maybe he could offer insights into why I was suddenly remembering that scene over and over again, suggest what I could do to dig out the last of the details that might tell me who the shadowy figure was and why it seemed so important to me I find out. Except, of course, I didn't. Because I knew why it was imperative I discover the truth.

Whoever ran that day killed that boy, a friend of mine I no longer remembered outside of these horrible moments of recollection that hit me like blows every single time. So, I owed it to that shadow to confront them with their guilt so I could maybe find a little peace. And get Victor the justice he deserved.

His life was stolen, our friendship, my connection to Vivian. Those losses were owed some kind of recompense.

"I'll make sure this gets to forensics," Dr. Aberstock said, crossing the room and pulling open a drawer, pulling out what looked like an evidence bag. I winced, whoops. But the doc happily deposited the evidence and sealed it, scrawling on it with a fat, black marker. "This might be telling, Fee, good catch. Here, let me show you." He set aside the bag and turned again, crossing to the bank of cold storage drawers, pulling one open and sliding the shelf out. I joined him with less enthusiasm, though I'd already seen Melina Canty's dead body, hadn't I? He had, as yet, to cut her open, no Y incision marring her pale chest, and he'd taped her eyes closed, thank goodness. Nothing like the pale milky emptiness of a dead person's gaze to give one the creeping heebie-jeebies.

"I've only had time for the preliminary analysis," he said, "but here. Look at this." He pointed with his gloved finger to a small, red puncture on her thigh, the faintest outline of darkness around it, like a bruise that hadn't had time to form completely. "Looks like an injection site to me."

"Was she maybe diabetic?" Look at me asking police questions like I deserved to carry the badge in my hand.

He shook his head. "Not sure, but this mark? Much too big for an insulin injection. And you see that bruise starting to form? Whatever the reason for the shot, the delivery was made hard enough to mark the skin." He seemed satisfied with my question, though. "So, we shall see if the trace I swabbed from her riding pants and the wound itself match the substance in your syringe."

"It could be the murder weapon?" Yes, me and conclusion jumping had a close, personal relationship. But I needed a win tonight.

He laughed like a big, happy cherub who really needed a red and fur-trimmed suit to finish the picture. "You're on the same track as me, Fee," he said. "And while I haven't done the full exam and don't quote me... well, I'm guessing we've discovered," so generous of him, he did most of the discovering, "our most possible cause of death, though how it triggered her end, what looks like cardiac arrest, I won't know until I finish the autopsy and get the chemical analysis back."

Fair enough.

"I can say," he said as he slid the shelf back into the wall and closed the small, steel door on the body, "that needle? Way bigger than anything I've used on a human."

Huh. "So, maybe more suited for a horse?"

He didn't answer with words, but the finger he laid on the side of his nose? Seriously.

He gave Kris Kringle a total run for the money.

CHAPTER FOURTEEN

My life had been so full of surprises, there were times I just couldn't seem to be shocked any longer. What with all the death, destruction, mayhem, attempts on my life, crazy circumstances and general unsettled chaos that revolved around me, Petunia's and the annex and, in general, the cozy little town that looked so sweet on the outside and seethed with such darkness on the inside… but I digress.

It wasn't that being shocked was the goal or anything. On the contrary, though a bit of excitement now and then wasn't a bad thing. But I considered myself rather jaded, to be honest, and anything of a startling nature felt rather humdrum when compared to stumbling over what amounted to more than the required number for a baseball team of corpses over the last three years.

Thing was, just because finding dead bodies didn't really do it for the old adrenaline lately, that didn't mean I wasn't able to be truly floored by the out-of-the-box. Though, as I stood, my mouth gaping open, my body frozen, the utter inability to react beyond the still, poleaxed state of my stuttering brain, I really shouldn't have been shocked to find Pamela Shard sitting in my dark kitchen, in my apartment beneath Petunia's, waiting for me when I got home from the morgue.

But I was shocked, by two things in particular. First was the fact that she'd snuck herself into my private residence and sat in the quiet stillness like a sneakthief until I arrived. So not like her to play small, overt, to hide herself. She'd never since I'd known her chosen to pretend she was anyone but who she'd become—a powerhouse of a woman, a seeker and writer of truths who made zero apology for the fact she would dig for a story until she got what she needed to ensure the world knew what actually happened and why it mattered.

I always respected and admired her for that stance, even if it put us at odds on occasion. But that courageous woman's spirit seemed to have gone. No, not completely. Faded, waned, like the moon turning to a sliver before it went dark. It was clear in everything about her she'd been through hell the last little while and was unable to hide it any longer. Because the second shock I processed was her physicality, her appearance. How pale, exhausted and tense she looked, worn to a nub. Not the woman I knew at all but a shadow of herself on the outside as she felt on the inside, the shift in her as palpable in the air, to my heart, as her face and body were to my eyes. Reminding me, with a start, of Olivia's present state so clearly, I did a double-take. As if, instead of residing with the wife of her dreams in an idyllic town in the middle of God's country, Pamela, like the mayor, appeared more like a seasoned battle veteran who was barely surviving PTSD while still struggling to keep herself alive in an active battle scenario.

What had that horrible family done to my friend? And who did I have to hurt to make it stop?

"Fee." She cleared her throat, the sound of her voice grating and harsh finally shattering my frozen state and sending me toward her as she stood uneasily from the stool where she'd been waiting, now wringing her hands, tears in her eyes. "Fee, please. Forgive me."

I threw myself at her, hugged her hard, rocking her a little while she wept on my shoulder. This was nuts and had gone way too far, these secrets kept. But when I released her and opened my mouth to say as such, she shook her head, eyes huge, sunken.

"I'm risking a lot, coming here." She choked on those words before her shoulders squared and the Pamela I knew better than this shade of a woman once powerful and reduced to ashes went on. "Sarah, Fee. She's innocent."

So, love for her niece was what it took to tear her

out of the smothering embrace of the Pattersons? "You have proof?"

Pamela fell still, face twisting, and I knew she didn't. Not that I cared. Like I'd said, Sarah's attachment to my (absolutely she was) friend meant she was on my list of people I had to protect against all comers. Did the newspaperwoman see that in my eyes? On my face? Or did she know me well enough she didn't have to doubt I'd do my best to see her brother's child wasn't convicted for a crime she didn't commit?

That was, if she didn't commit it. Sigh.

"Lenny and I, we're estranged," Pamela said. "Just never saw eye-to-eye, you know? But I adore Sarah. Fee, she might have a temper, but she's not a murderer." She seemed to flicker into her old self a moment, a smile twisting her lips. "You get having a temper, right?"

Smartypants.

"Sarah's my only real family." Pamela sagged to the stool again, shoulders rounded, looking even more defeated than ever.

"What about Aundrea?" I didn't mean to use that question as a weapon or to prod her for information, but she flinched in response anyway. Too much of an investigator herself to forget just what brought us together in the first place. Our mutual love of busybodying wasn't lost on me, either.

"There's a reason Sarah's being targeted." She swallowed, wiped at her mouth with a trembling hand. "And Robert has his instructions, Fee. If I fall out of line…" That was real fear on her face. I knew Pamela had faced down some truly terrible things in her time, working for *The Boston Globe* years ago. There was no way she would have survived in her job if she'd not been able to look such terror in the eye and tell it to go to hell. Apparently, she'd lost that ability.

The Pattersons again. This was getting old.

"Let me help," I said, but she was already shaking her head, standing up, heading for the stairs.

"Fee, you *can't*." She stressed that word so strongly I stopped in my tracks again. "You just can't. Okay?" I refused to nod my acknowledgment to which my friend sighed. "Listen, I know, I do. I get it. I understand you more than anyone. You can't let this go. Dog with a bone." She gagged on the bark of a laugh, almost in tears once more. Now I was really worried about her. This had gone from cutting me out of a wedding to, quite frankly, the worst sort of mysteriously threatening horror movie I'd rather not watch alone at night, thanks.

What was going on?

"Please," Pamela said, one foot on the steps, still dressed, I realized, in the suit she must have worn to the wedding, pale blue that didn't do anything for her washed-out complexion, even the boutonniere on her jacket now crushed and limp as if my hug had done it in as much as anything. "This is my fault. I encouraged her to come here, to take the opportunity when it was offered. I thought it was a good thing for her. But I was wrong, Fee. I was so wrong." She shivered. "About a lot of things." Was that guilt? Regret? Mixed with the deepest anxiety I'd ever seen. She flushed then, the blotchy kind of patchwork redness that usually happened as a result of an ugly cry, though she was tearless this time. "Just do what you can for Sarah?"

She didn't wait for me to respond, disappearing on running feet up the steps and I simply stood there, listening to the sound of her footfalls as they retreated to the swinging door to the kitchen.

Pamela didn't use the front entry. She went out the back. Which meant she really was hiding she'd been here.

I wanted to call Crew, then remembered he wasn't here. Thought about Dad. Paused yet again. If things were this bad, should I involve him? And then I snorted. Silly. Dad was already as deeply embedded in whatever this giant mess was as me. More so maybe, if the truth of Fiona Doyle's disappearance was tied to the Pattersons as he and I—and her father, Malcolm Murray—believed.

I hadn't thought much about the missing woman in the last little while, the summer's business overwhelming. And I hadn't heard again from her mother, the lovely Irishwoman, Siobhan, not since she'd called to tell me she thought her daughter was still alive.

Funny how even the biggest, most intriguing mysteries could fall to the wayside when life gets in the road. Though I had to admit, the fact Dad had spent all these years—three decades worth—

searching for the other Fiona, cut me a bit of slack. If my father, the master of busybodies I'd learned my own nose poking skills from, hadn't been able to uncover the truth in all that time surely, I was allowed a bit of leeway in my own investigations.

I was wrapped up in that particular line of thought when my phone rang and I meeped in surprise when it did. Okay, so I could be startled, awesome. I glanced at the screen before heading to the door in a hurry, trusting the person on the other end wasn't the sort to be hasty with her commands.

Liz didn't seem the type to overreact. So, her terse, *Get to the sheriff's office*, was all I needed to send me scurrying.

CHAPTER FIFTEEN

I stormed into the office, noting the absence of a receptionist—Crew had been struggling to keep anyone at the desk, not to mention the fact it was getting on to 9PM, so it wasn't a big stretch to see the empty seat—as an aside while I hustled past the swinging gate partitioning the front entry from the bullpen.

Just in time to hear Robert's ridiculous pronouncement as he stood in the center of the room, hands on hips, rounded belly jutting outward, idiotic mustache making him look like a 70's porn star gone to pot. "I'm officially charging Sarah Shard with the murder of Melina Canty."

The fact he felt like he had to make such a pronouncement spoke volumes. Before anyone else could comment, protest or otherwise assure him he was a total and utter moron, I huffed to a halt and did the honors.

"I take it Dr. Aberstock called," I said. "Named it an official homicide?" I hadn't been home long and while we'd discussed it between us, the doc liked to be thorough before making a call like that one. Surely the fifteen minutes it had taken me to drive home and the five-minute conversation I'd had with Pamela hadn't given the doc enough time to complete a complex and in-depth autopsy?

Robert scowled at me, and I noted as he did the peeking glare I received from his girlfriend. The other half of Rosebert's pinched expression and her total lack, at this point, to try to hide her dislike for me was actually welcome. I hated hypocrites. Nice to know exactly where I stood with Rose.

"Don't think you can interfere," she snapped at me, ducking around him, arms crossing over her chest. Wait, what was she wearing? A uniform shirt? Dear god in heaven, had Crew lost his mind and made her a deputy, too? But there was no badge, no gun and, as I again made mental note of the empty chair in reception, I realized the role she'd been playing lately. Answering phones didn't make her a cop. Though, to be honest, possessing a badge barely made me one. Still.

I outranked her. Snort.

"Well?" I glanced at Jill who shook her head. She was still lead on this case, her frustration with her coworker as obvious as Rose's dislike.

"We're still waiting on the doc and COD," she said. "Though, he did say to proceed with the expectation it was foul play." She winced then, part apology, part disgust with herself she was giving Robert any kind of fodder for his little one-man show.

His black fur facial covering twitched, piggy eyes alight with all the support he needed. "Case closed," he said.

Please, just someone shoot him already and put him—and the rest of us—out of misery.

"Because you have proof," I said, joining Liz who, I only now noticed, perched on the edge of Jill's desk, behind her and out of the way. I purposely tapped into her droll, dry tone, the one I admired so much, instead of my usual attempt to be crisp, professional, gravelly like Dad and Crew. Found I liked it so much better. Liz's barely-there grin told me either I was crushing it or making a fool of myself but I had to trust I was doing this right so I went on. "A murder weapon." I thought of the syringe. "Some kind of material evidence." I glanced over my shoulder where Sarah sat, head in her hands, in the nearest cell. "A confession, perhaps?"

Robert spluttered, face turning red. "She's guilty," he said. "They fought just before the woman was killed."

"So, the argument I witnessed between Gretchen, Charlie and Melina meant nothing?" I shrugged, loving this persona and secretly squealing in delight deep inside while I held myself together through sheer will and the need to destroy my cousin.

Robert floundered while Jill exhaled slowly like she'd been holding that breath in under the same level of willpower I employed. "As I said." She met my eyes. "Several times." Jill's posture shifted from tense and rigid to more relaxed, though, so even if I could never convince Robert he was truly an arse I had, at least, given my friend the respite she needed to keep from shooting him in the face. Though I doubted anyone—aside from Rose—would care if she did. Even Liz would give Jill a pass, I was sure of it. Public service, that.

"This is ridiculous," I said. "And so like you, Robert. So, tell me." I held his gaze, saw the darkness surface, pushed back against it until he retreated just enough, I knew I'd won while making him even more dangerous at the same time and not really caring just then. "Who's really paying your check, cousin? Because it's clearly not the Reading Sheriff's department. Stinks like collusion if you ask me."

Liz's interjection caught me by surprise. "You have proof of that, Deputy Fleming?" I glanced at her while she stared at Robert herself, suddenly looking more predator than woman. "Because if you do, the FBI would be happy to investigate."

"How dare you threaten my Robertkins." Rose wasn't doing him any favors and for the first time, I caught his annoyance with her, the flare of fury aimed at the woman who just emasculated him in front of all of us. Had to cut deep, seeing his private parts handed over to a bunch of women by the one person in the world he likely thought had his back. Rose didn't notice, rushing on in a heated tirade. "He's the only person in this town who actually understands how things are run. So, you listen up, Fiona Fleming." She shook her index finger at me while I felt a grin spread over my face, humorless and full of disdain. "You'll just back off if you know what's good for you. Right, Robert?" She stepped back, arm sliding through his, still missing the jaw-clench, the sullen rage.

Whatever. I'd do a happy dance if these two imploded. I just didn't want to have to witness it.

"Excuse me." I turned when Sarah spoke, distracted from the unfolding show, to find she had come to the edge of the cell, hands grasping the bars, still dressed in her riding clothes, her helmet on the bench left behind her. "I'd like to talk to my aunt."

Robert's black rage returned, and he lunged toward her, shocking everyone, including me—yup, still possible after all. "Your little auntie is in her own hot water," he snarled, voice low but still audible. "Don't think Pamela is in any position to help you."

Sarah staggered back, face twisting in anxious worry. "What? What are you talking about? Where is she? I want to see her!"

I grasped Robert's arm without thinking, pulling him away from Sarah. He snarled, an animal-like sound, glaring into my eyes while we stood toe-to-toe, his face so close to mine I could smell his disgusting breath.

"You have to know this isn't going to end well

for you," I said. "Don't be an idiot, Robert. The Pattersons might own you now, but their day in court is coming and when it does, you'll go down with them." Maybe an empty threat. Maybe not. But regardless, it got a reaction.

Robert jerked his arm free of my grasp. "We'll see who ends up at the bottom of the pile when everything shakes out."

That sounded suspiciously like he knew something was pending and wanted to rub my face in it. "Meaning?"

He caught himself, backed off, wiping at his mouth with one hand, shaking his head. "I can't wait to see you fall." Robert spun on Liz, close enough to be uncomfortable, but she didn't flinch or even show a modicum of concern he was an inch from her when he spoke. "The FBI wasn't invited into this investigation so the next time you want to interfere or make threats, you'd better have some kind of permission to back yourself up."

She shrugged. "Actually, I was invited. By your boss." Liz tilted her head to one side, as if observing a rather uninteresting cockroach she was considering squashing under her shoe. "Come at me, Deputy Carlisle."

He was going to. Seriously, the clueless jackass was actually going to. I saw it in his face, in his body language, about a second before Rose lurched forward and grasped his arm, tugging on him. Enough of a distraction to break his state of deluded darkness and shake off the need he clearly had to put her in her place.

Robert stormed out, Rose on his heels, leaving the three of us to watch them both go with varying degrees of holy crap what was that. Liz recovered first, exhaling slowly while Jill nodded as if the agent had spoken.

No words necessary. He was at the edge of a cliff of his own making and, one way or another, Robert was going to crash and burn. Not if.

When.

I turned to Sarah who still clutched at the bars, her cheeks wet with tears.

"Aunt Pam?" She didn't seem to care she was in a jail cell, only thinking about Pamela. That gave her big points in my books.

"Sarah, do you have an alibi for the half-hour or so after I left you?" No need to remind her I was escorted out of the facility.

Sarah sagged, shook her head, resting her forehead against the metal bars. "I was in SuSu's stall, grooming her, then I went to my room. But I didn't see anyone." She hesitated a moment before adding the next bit of information. "The stall where you found Melina? It's next to Susu's."

That didn't look good and apparently, Sarah was well aware of it. "Cameras?" There had to be something to prove her innocence.

She perked a bit then shook her denial once more. "There is security footage of the main walkways, but nothing in the stalls."

And giant windows for the horses to use in every

one. An easy out if Sarah had wanted to exit without being seen. Still, it gave us somewhere to start. If we could track her progress and create a timeline, maybe we could exonerate her while finding the real killer.

I turned to Jill who waved. "Already on it," she said. "The footage is being compiled."

"I hated her." Sarah hissed that, shaking a little. "But I didn't want her dead." She glared at her hands tightly wound around the metal in front of her. "My best revenge against Melina was making the team, Fee. Her dying? Took away my chance to prove to her I was the rider she said I couldn't be."

So, her beef with Melina was about training? "She used to be your coach?"

Sarah nodded once, a jerking motion that looked more like an attempt at denial than acknowledgment of fact. "For five years," she said, snuffled. Wiped at her nose with the back of her hand. "Then she suddenly told me I was a waste of her time and dumped me."

Whoops. "And took on Violet instead?"

Sarah didn't comment on that. Didn't have to. "I was lucky Alphonse was willing to take me on."

I heard the door open behind me, asked one last question. "Who would want her dead?"

"Who wouldn't?" It was the very man Sarah just mentioned who answered, joining us, long legs carrying him in big strides to my side. "Sarah, my dear, are you all right?" He spun on me, fury on his face. "Surely this is unnecessary. It's clear she's innocent of any crime."

He had to have been dealing with Robert up until now, his animosity so powerful I could only chalk that level of frustration up to being manhandled by my inept cousin.

"You have an alternative suspect in mind, Mr. Brunbaugh?" I wasn't going to just let Sarah off the hook, despite agreeing with her new coach. That wasn't my job. It was Jill's.

So was questioning Alphonse, to be honest, though I imagined she'd already had a go at him. And knew I was right when he jabbed a finger at her.

"As I told Deputy Wagner," he said, "you should be looking at that debutante, Emile Reis."

The handsome European investor? "Why is that?"

"Because," Alphonse said, looking offended at the fact he had to repeat himself to me, another lowly deputy, "they were lovers and she rejected him." He wiggled his impressive eyebrows at me. "Publicly."

CHAPTER SIXTEEN

Despite the fact Jill had already interviewed Emile Reis, she had zero issue with me taking the drive to the White Valley Lodge to have a chat with him the next morning.

"You know I'm not offended, Fee," she told me, her aggravation over Robert fading as she set Sarah free into Alphonse's custody with their assurance she would be available for further questioning, if necessary, and remain at the equestrian center. I'd hugged the young rider, felt her shiver against me, accepted her smile of thanks—though it was my deputy friend who'd released her and deserved the gratitude—before letting her go in favor of talking to the other suspects. After informing her Pamela had personally asked me to help. That seemed to help the young woman's worry, but I was sure she'd be doing her best to reach her aunt on her own as soon as she was free to do so. "If anything, redundancy in interviews is a favorite of mine." Jill waved me off. "You might ask a question in a way I didn't. Please, don't hesitate."

"You do realize no one will actually speak to me." Yeah, still bitter about it.

But Jill wasn't having that. "I understand, I really do." She and Liz both eye-rolled like this was old news to them. "You might think they have some kind of grudge but trust me. No one enjoys talking to law enforcement. Just keep at it, be firm and you'll get through."

I wasn't so sure as I parked in the main lot at the lodge just before 10AM and forced myself to walk with my head up and shoulders back into the lobby. Not just because I was certain I was about to be shut down, but partially due to the fact every time I came to this place these days it just hurt my heart. Reminding me endlessly of the schism between me and Alicia and Jared.

Jill had supplied me with Emile's room number, so I bypassed the front desk and headed across the big, white lobby with the shining crystal chandeliers overhead, taking the elevator to the top floor and the suite our European visitor had claimed for his own. I honestly already had my back up over the whole investigation thing, and knowing the arrogant, rich dude had, ultimately, rejected Daisy in favor of Vivian French (yes, I remembered that much from the last time I'd seen him that fateful February and no one rejected my Day over someone like the Queen of Wheat, the ass), wasn't doing him any favors.

I knocked on his door, a bit more firmly than necessary, choosing to trust Jill's assessment of the situation and take her advice to heart.

He answered almost immediately, though from the faint frown on his handsome face, he wasn't exactly happy to see me. The company he was keeping might have been the reason why. Maybe he'd already been frowning before I got there? Okay, not exactly fair to blame the gorgeous and perfectly clad Vivian who stood by the far window, her pale, blonde hair almost transparent in the morning sunlight a pretty good artificial match for his naturally icy coloring, observing as I pretty much just pushed my way into the room and ignored her.

I'd thought he and Daisy looked amazing together. But I wasn't above admitting he and Vivian could have come from the same frozen tundra where they only made beautiful white people.

"Mr. Reis," I said, flashing the badge on my belt. "Deputy Fiona Fleming, Reading Sheriff's Department. I have a few questions about the death of Melina Canty."

He nodded and stepped aside as if I hadn't just bullied my way past him, gesturing for me to join Vivian in the living room area of the suite. My sneakers slipped over the lush, furry carpet, shaggy white and so soft I felt my feet sink just a bit. The matching pale sofa and two elegant armchairs surrounded a glass and chrome coffee table overlooking the valley below. Picturesque, especially with the private infinity pool, the most unrealistic but brilliant shade of blue that matched Emile's eyes (focus, Fee), spilling its endlessly cycling waters over the edge as if the world were finite and the flat earthers weren't nuts.

A faint pain between my shoulder blades gave me a tweak of temper as I hunched against my mix of emotions. Not just Emile, but Vivian's presence, the way she always stared at me like I was intruding on her life instead of the other way around. Okay, so I was intruding. But I had good reason. And while we weren't exactly enemies these days, no way was she my friend, not like we'd been when we were kids, and I saved her life.

The same day we watched her brother drown.

"Fee." She nodded her acknowledgment but instead of making me feel better, it instead just made things worse. Queen of Wheat, indeed.

"What's going on between you and Olivia?" Blunt enough for you, Vivs?

She didn't answer, expression already flat going decidedly chilly. "You'll find out soon enough." She focused her icy attention on Emile. "Thank you for the lovely breakfast," she said, going to his side, kissing both of his cheeks. "I need to go. But I'll see you again before you leave?"

He held her hands, nodded down at her with a faint, sad smile. "My dear Vivian," he said with enough of an accent he sounded deliciously foreign to match that tall, blond handsomeness of his. "Always a delight."

She left without another word, sashaying her slim suited self to the door before letting herself out. I did my best not to feel jealous (she was gorgeous, I wasn't above admitting it) or annoyed at the way she always seemed able to wind me up without doing much of anything.

Lucky Emile got to deal with the leftovers.

But when I indelicately broached the topic of his supposed affair with Melina Canty, he flatly denied it, his entire being rejecting the idea, to the point I actually believed him.

"Trust me, Deputy Fleming," he said, accent thicker as his temper got the best of him, "the last person on earth I would be interested in for a romantic relationship was Melina Canty. Please, don't misconstrue my words." He waved one big hand at me, a large gold and diamond ring on his right hand catching the sunlight before he ran it through his thick, blond hair, then down the side of his cheek, the faint scratching sound of his skin over the hint of a beard loud in the quiet room. "While Melina and I didn't agree on her idea of training for the young hopefuls, I didn't wish her ill. Only failure."

"Why is that?" Quite the thing to say if he was a sponsor.

"Because her methods of winning wouldn't pass the full scrutiny of the Olympic committee." He was blunt enough. "And while I have no proof of misdeeds, I can tell you I personally witnessed her tampering with one of the horses."

Tampering? "Involving a syringe of some kind?" Did the needle she meant for a horse somehow get injected into her own body? "That's a pretty big accusation, Mr. Reis. Especially without proof."

He shrugged, big hands spread wide, frowning. "Thus, the reason I have, as yet, to pull my support of the rider's trial efforts or make a formal report to the committee. I can tell you, however, any suggestion of Ms. Canty and myself being intimate is greatly exaggerated." He hesitated before sighing. "I am, I'm afraid, enamored of another. And she, at this time, does not return my affections." He met my eyes with his pale ones. "Though I live in hope she might eventually change her mind and can only linger in this town and offer her my continuing devotion."

Okay, holy wow. In that instant, I knew exactly who he was courting and, suddenly sad for her, wondered why Vivian would lead him on like that. Because it had to be her. And while his refusal to take no for an answer could have been creepy, I felt my heart—enraptured with Crew Turner as it was and far too romantically inclined for my own good these days—sigh a little, "Ah!" of unrequited love. Especially for someone like Vivian who, I knew, was so emotionally shut down it was likely he'd pine away for her forever.

Tragic, really. He seemed truly heartbroken.

But not my problem at the moment. "Can you tell me where you went shortly after I left the argument?" Again, not bringing up the escorted-out thing and Emile was far too much of a gentleman to comment otherwise. Yeah, I was kind of warming up to him.

"I was on the phone, as it happens," he said, fishing it out and showing me the time stamp on the call he mentioned. "For the better part of an hour, actually. I didn't even know Melina had died until your Deputy Wagner came to talk to me."

Okay then, alibi achieved. I'd be checking on that phone number, though, because he could easily have dialed one of his own numbers, had someone answer and simply left the connection open to create doubt. And yet, it seemed like a big effort for something that felt to me more like a crime of passion. Then again, I still didn't know for sure the syringe was a murder weapon.

Had to call Dr. Aberstock.

I wrapped up quickly, thanking him for his patience, only to have him stop me on my way out.

"I beg you," Emile said, "a favor, Miss Fleming?"

Weird. "If you want me to keep your name out of the paper or something, there's not much I can do."

He denied that request with a wry twist of his lips. "I assure you I've been enmeshed in the negative attention of the media in the past and likely will be in the future. No, it's of a more personal nature. I know you are friends with her, and I was hoping…" he left it hanging as if unable to finish.

Wow. He wanted me to put in a good word with Vivian? Did she tell him we were friends? Because nope. I considered his request, though, while doubting my word would do him any good.

I didn't get to say one way or the other. Emile paused, flinched. "And yet, that is too much to ask. Forgive me. I've overstepped. Good day to you, deputy." He offered that last with a small smile and closed the door behind me.

CHAPTER SEVENTEEN

Sarah's room looked like no one lived in it, the kind of tidy neatness that made me second guess my own life choices when it came to the clutter that was my closet. I sighed while I stood back and stared at the rather OCD organization of color-coded breeches, golf shirts, white shirts, black jackets and polished tall boots that filled one end, the bare selection of street clothes on the shelf and hanging sadly on the other side evidence the young rider did little that wasn't to do with horses.

Not much of a life, but then again, who was I to judge? She was doing what she loved, right? And if it wasn't for Crew and Daisy, would I even have a social life?

Pots, kettles and calling out the black, Fleming.

Liz looked up from the drawer she was examining on the other side of the room with a grin. "Kid's neat as a pin."

"Tell me about it." I removed my gloves and stuffed them into my pocket. We'd been over every inch of the room and found nothing to do with a syringe or any kind of injectable. This was my third look in her closet, just to be thorough, though truthfully, I was kind of in awe of Sarah's commitment to tidiness and simply had to have another peek.

Liz closed the drawer with a solid thud, her own gloves neatly and efficiently removed tucked away in her jacket as she continued to scan the room with her gaze, refusing to quit until she was sure there was nothing to find. The kind of tenacity I admired and liked to think I possessed myself. Dog with a bone? She'd accused me of as much. Guilty. But even Liz finally pursed her lips in defeat. "That's that, then. There's nothing here to connect Miss Shard to the syringe you found." Did she sound disappointed? I couldn't bring myself to believe it was due to a lack of evidence against Sarah, but instead a cop's reaction to a fruitless search for the truth and justice for the victim.

What, me romanticizing? Go figure.

"And still no proof it was the COD." I'd called Dr. Aberstock earlier, after leaving Emile to mourn his unanswered affections, and before Liz asked me to join her in this little exploration of Sarah's personal belongings. No cause of death yet, and no fingerprints on the syringe to point to who'd had it in their possession prior to my discovery.

I suppressed a little shiver of uncomfortableness, couldn't help but feel like I was being a voyeur digging around in Sarah's stuff like this, despite knowing it was part of the job. Weird to rifle through the girl's underwear and bras, her personal photos—how few there were of them—knowing she'd likely go through the whole space and have to "fix" everything we'd touched. I knew I'd be upset and creeped out if I had to endure such a search and I was about as far from OCD as anyone.

The door opened without preamble, Robert lurking on the other side. He'd followed us from the parking lot, furious and fuming over Jill releasing Sarah, making it utterly clear as he rambled on in a tirade I mostly ignored and barely caught the gist of all the way here that he was going to do his best to ensure she paid for the crime I knew she didn't commit. I hated leaving her outside with him while Liz and I conducted the search, but we had no other options, not when he came to a halt in the hallway, still muttering his protests, while we knocked, and Sarah appeared.

She'd let us in without argument, cooperating fully, a good sign as far as I was concerned. Not biased or anything. Though it was possible her confidence in allowing us to look through her things meant if she was the killer, she'd hidden the evidence elsewhere or disposed of it already.

Doubt, you sucked.

But, despite knowing Robert would spend the time Liz and I took doing our search making a total ass and bother of himself, there was no way I was letting him in the room to look with us. Even if three bodies weren't a huge inconvenience in the rather small space, I couldn't put him planting evidence past him, could I? Besides, it wasn't up to me, in the end. Liz simply closed the door in his face, the unhappy Alphonse appearing to act as a shield for Sarah while we did our duty.

Apparently, Robert had finally gotten impatient enough to challenge my FBI agent friend (yup, claimed her. Are you really surprised?) "What did you find?"

Like I was going to tell him anything. And yet… "Nothing." I shrugged. "The room is clean."

He took one step past the threshold, stopped by the sudden move Liz made to block him. Just an equal and opposite step in his direction, but enough to freeze him in his unhappy tracks.

"You didn't look hard enough." He squinted into the well-lit space, glaring around as if we'd purposely avoided doing what we came here to do.

"Sure," Liz said in her droll drawl. "Because this huge place has so many hiding spaces."

Snort.

Robert didn't meet her eyes, choosing to focus on me, bless him. "If she gets off because of your incompetence, Fanny—"

I closed the distance between us faster than he could finish, this time getting in his face. He actually stumbled back, heels catching on the threshold strip at the door, and it was clear from his expression as he recovered he had added that little affront to his long, long list of marks against me. Let him. I was over it.

"I have no idea what your problem is," I snarled, low and private, "but I'm done, Robert. If the Pattersons own you, fine. None of my business. But pinning a murder on an innocent girl, that's a low move, even for you." He winced just enough I knew I'd gotten through. Guilt, from him? No way. Wasn't buying it. Still, he was listening and that was a rarity, so I went on. Would have anyway. "Stop being a damned wild card and an ass and maybe you'll get a little respect for once. Until then, stay the hell out of the way or I'll take Agent Michaud up on her offer to have the FBI look into you." That was real fear in his eyes. Point Fleming. Made me sad, in a way, since he was blood and all. But no accounting for who I was related to. "Back off, Robert."

He did, turning and leaving, while my chest unclenched but the part of me that knew he was a danger to himself and others—mostly others—unable to breathe a sigh of relief.

My dear, darling asshat cousin Robert was a ticking time bomb and when he finally exploded?

Yeah, guess who'd be in the line of fire?

I spent the rest of the day with Liz and Jill, digging through the private lives of the suspects, gaining a new respect for the life of a police officer and FBI agent. Not everyone—read, no one—was as tidy as Sarah and I found myself sorting through dirty socks, underwear that might or might not have taken on a life of their own (looking at you Jimmy Hogan), piled-up trash marred with tissues loaded with lipstick and, oddly, a gazillion chocolate bar wrappers (sweet tooth, there, Violet? This must have been the source of Sarah's fat comment when I'd first met them both) that argued such an addiction couldn't go hand in hand with her tiny size.

Metabolism much?

By the time we wrapped up the room-by-room search, our task aided by the meager two forensics techs Reading's Sheriff's Department had at their disposal part-time, I was sore from bending, tired of other people's crap and ready to go home and hide in the basement.

Didn't get to, though, not until I helped Jill and Liz fill out the reports on the searches in triplicate. Hunched over the end of Jill's desk while Robert sat back with both feet on his, hands laced behind his head, refusing to help. Not that we wanted his help.

When I finally made it home to Petunia's, I was grateful it was mid-September and late enough in the season I didn't have to deal with the overflow of tourists the summer brought. A glance at the roster told me we had a full house, that Daisy was on top of things—where was my bestie, anyway? Hadn't seen her in days—and that I could retreat without too much guilt to the sanctuary of my apartment, kick off my sneakers and maybe enjoy a dinner of ice cream and angst over whatever in me thought I could make it as a cop.

Dad was right about me not pursuing law enforcement, but not for the reasons he named. I thought the paper shuffle for this place was bad. It was a wonder anyone caught any bad guys with all the stupid forms they had to file just to look through another person's belongings in a fruitless search for evidence of what we still didn't know for sure was murder.

Yup, I was in a great mood. Thanks for asking.

As I stomped down the steps, my fat, farting pug plodding one foot at a time in front of me, I was deeply implanted in the spiraling annoyance I felt toward the job I'd thought I wanted. So much so, I missed Petunia's first huffed growl of surprise, her faint bark of inquiry, though as I came to a halt because she stopped and literally would have tripped me over her bulk if I kept going, I realized she was the only warning I had I wasn't alone.

The light switch illuminated my visitor, sitting at my kitchen island, while I held my breath against the need to scream and run for the hills. For the second night in a row, I had an uninvited guest.

Like Pamela Shard, Charlie Chaswick didn't look like he was there for a social call.

CHAPTER EIGHTEEN

Yup, screaming was at the top of my to-do list, except Charlie hastily stood and waved off my inhaled intent to alert the entire household to the fact he'd broken into my apartment.

He looked suitably concerned by my reaction I held onto the shreds of decorum remaining me while he hastily spoke.

"Please, Miss—sorry, Deputy Fleming." He got points for that quick about-face correction. "I'm not here to hurt you, I swear. I have information and I couldn't deliver it out in the open."

Didn't justify lurking in the dark in my private space, but I'd cut him a wee bit of slack. The last person (prior to Pamela, that was) I'd found hiding out in my place had turned out to be a stalker and a kind of ally who had almost died trying to save me and solve the murder of a model. Mila Martin might have been in prison for her attack on Frederick Newmark, but there was enough of a feeling of familiarity to this invasion I figured I needed to up my personal security.

No, it wasn't lost on me I had done my own B&E only a day before, and maybe I shouldn't have been pointing fingers and feeling all huffy and offended by the intrusion. Then again, I'd broken into a giant complex, not Charlie's living room.

I'd let him have a pass, though. Only if his supposed information had merit and led me where I needed to go, namely to the person responsible for Melina Canty's death.

"Spill it," I snapped, already on a tightrope and wishing Jill had relented and given me a gun. Then again, I may have, instead of listening to Charlie tell me what he knew, been calling that self-same deputy and confessing I'd shot him with the afore-mentioned weapon. So, maybe she was right to keep the projectiles away from me.

"Look into Gretchen Latrell," he said, voice low and heavy with mystery.

"Why is that?" I was done with people giving me half-answers and keeping the juiciest bits to themselves. Pamela, Alicia, Jared, Vivian, Olivia... the list was long and impressive and frustrating. This character I barely knew? He didn't get to follow in their footsteps.

"I can't say." Charlie looked nervous enough,

though of my reaction to him or the present situation he found himself in I didn't know. Sure, he was risking his job being here, he'd told me as much at the center. But was there more to his reticence? Better be because loss of employment didn't trump uncovering a murderer.

Supposed murderer. Sigh. I really needed Dr. Aberstock to tell me one way or the other before my brain made up my mind for me.

"Can't or won't?" Petunia had approached him without my consent, sniffing at his sneakers, whuffing softly under her breath. The line of slightly darker fur down the center of her back stood at attention, her normally cinnamon bun curl of a tail hanging low. She didn't like or trust him, a rarity for her, though she'd lost her utter happy-go-lucky no matter what with everyone she met when Robert tried to drown her. Still, it wasn't often she reacted this way to strangers, so I needed to trust her instincts.

But Charlie didn't seem to care about the pug's reaction, just his own skin, apparently. He shuffled past her, heading toward me while I backed off and circled, making sure I faced him the whole time, thinking about the drawer of knives and how far it was in comparison to the stable hand. He appeared innocent enough but one just never knew.

"I'm not a threat to you, Deputy Fleming," he said. "I swear. And I have an alibi." He stuck his hands in the pockets of his jeans, flushing. "I was with Violet in the east stable tack room."

"You told Deputy Wagner this?" I held my ground at last, Petunia sinking to her fat butt to look up at him with her tongue hanging out. Had she decided he was okay after all, and I could relax myself? Funny how I took the word of my portly canine companion over that of the man himself. But she was an excellent judge of character that Petunia.

"I told her part of it," he said. "Violet didn't want her to know." He sounded like he was used to being treated like he didn't matter. "But I'm telling you because it proves we're both innocent."

"You have proof?" I watched him slide a small flash drive out of his pocket and set it on my kitchen island.

"I do," he said. "I usually make copies of any video, just in case, before deleting the evidence." Again that softly angsty tone that meant it bothered him he had to take such steps. Why was he with her, then, if she treated him like crap? "That will show me and Violet entering the tack room where we stayed for about forty-five minutes. We didn't even know Melina was dead until about fifteen minutes after we were done."

Okay, fine. "I'll give this to Deputy Wagner," I said. "But I could use a solid reason to look into Gretchen so I'm not just fishing, Charlie."

He looked like he wanted to say more but instead just bobbed a nod at me and dashed.

I could have followed him, thought about it, in fact. Drew a few breaths to steady myself while looking around my apartment and wondering what kind of safety measures I could install to keep people from sneaking down here and scaring the crap out of me. Had a rough blueprint of heat-seeking lasers and a giant siren with flashing red lights and a cyborg voice telling them they were dead in five, four, three, two, one playing out in my head when the door at the top of the stairs opened and yet another random helped themselves to my private quarters.

Okay, so my next visitor wasn't so random and at least I was home when Vivian French descended the steps and paused at the bottom, observing me as if she didn't know why she was there and was pretty positive I was about to argue about her setting one high heel in my space.

Instead, I sagged against the counter and sighed. "Yes, Vivian?" I had a million questions for her, too, but couldn't seem to generate any in the wake of the last two days I'd endured. You know what? She could keep her freaking secrets. The whole damned town could just burn to the ground, and I'd have been okay with it right about then.

"Fee." Vivian's shoe tapped delicately on the tile floor as she took that last step, stopping again, this time with her face, so poised and blank, showing emotion that bordered on sorrow.

I immediately thought about Emile Reis and her visit with him, his clear and present adoration of her. But, when Vivian spoke while I wondered why she would come to me, of all people, for love advice, she shattered my assumptions.

"I'm going to run for mayor," she said, proving

yet again that yes, I could be surprised, thank you, and that these sorts of shocks really weren't good for the old Fleming ticker, just so you know. "And I need to know I have your support."

Reaction #1: why would I support her? Reaction #2: is this what the whole meeting in Olivia's office had been about? Reaction #3: could I really see Vivian French as the next mayor of the cutest town in America?

I'm sure all three of those flashed over my face while I choked on a half-laugh that had zero connection to amusement and everything with flabbergasted holy heck in a handbasket of trouble that had nothing to do with me.

"There's a great deal going on you don't know about," she said then, not exactly hasty but without the usual methodical and icy tone she typically employed when she chose to speak to me. "I know you want answers, and I have some for you, but only if I know I can trust you. But first, Fee, first." She swallowed. "You have to trust me."

I caught myself nodding. Not because I did trust her, but because she stood there, open and raw and vulnerable, and let me see just how anxious she really was before shutting off her emotional exposure like a tap being twisted with the kind of force that stripped the threads.

"You're in the Patterson's camp," I said, despite myself.

Rage flared, a reaction I wasn't expecting. Vivian lunged at me, that particular emotion making her normally beautiful face rather hideous for a moment.

"I'm there for a reason," she snarled, voice harsh, humming with anger. "Behind enemy lines. Doing what I have to, Fiona Fleming. What you can't." She drew a shaking breath, visibly pulling herself together. She smoothed the front of her dress with both hands, trembling just enough I caught it as her fingers slipped down the shining ivory fabric. "I need you to promise me you'll support me. No matter what happens. Even if you're furious with me. Fee. I need you." She dropped her hands to her sides. "Please."

Okay, Vivian French pleading with me to have her back had not been on my agenda for today and, unlike anything else she'd tried, was a shoo-in to trigger my acceptance.

"I need to know what's going on Viv," I said. "I can't help you if I'm in the dark."

She hesitated, the silence between us so heavy and thick I felt my throat tightening from it. Even as memory took over, the worst timing ever, and I was again on the dock, on that fateful, overcast day, holding her sobbing and soaked form in my arms while her brother sank under the lake's surface.

Did she know who the shadow figure had been? The one who'd watched Victor drown only to run away? My phone rang, the cheery ringtone that told me Crew was calling. Vivian didn't wait for me to answer, her lips in a tight line. And, as I pressed the green button to accept his call, she left without another word.

CHAPTER NINETEEN

"Hello, beautiful," my fiancé said, still sounding sad and tired, but, as always, my hero and the man I loved more every day. "Tell me everything."

We hadn't connected the night before like we'd planned, and I was only just realizing that now. Had I said I'd call and failed to? Had he planned to phone and forgot or was distracted by what kept him in California? Didn't matter, not now. Not when he was there, on the other end of the line, available for me, wanting to support me any way he could.

I sat on the stool in my kitchen and filled him in, including Robert's meeting with who I guessed was Marie Patterson, Pam and Charlie's visits (wince) and my last visitor and Vivian's odd request.

Crew listened carefully, making the right noises at

the right times as I spoke at length, keeping his judgments to himself despite the fact I knew it was likely the vein in his forehead was standing out and if I could have seen his eye there'd be a tic going off like no one's business under it.

"I'm not so sure backing Vivian is a good idea." He had to start there, didn't he? "Fee, there have been some pretty big pressures building in the office for months and Olivia's been acting weirder than usual. I have no idea what's going on, but we both know the Pattersons are behind it." Crew paused, exhaled heavily into the phone. "I've been meaning to talk to you about my future as sheriff in Reading. I'm being pushed out, have spent so much energy pushing back the last few years I'm tired, Fee." I knew he was under strain, but I had no idea he was this close to quitting. Did I blame him? Weird time to have this talk, and yet, that was us, wasn't it? Not exactly a typical couple and I wouldn't have it any other way. "I'm thinking about taking your dad's offer to work for Fleming Investigations and wash my hands of the mess." Right. Dad offered him a job a while back. Part of me had thought that was a joke. It would make Crew my employee, right? Not awkward or anything. Clearly, Dad had been serious, enough Crew was still thinking about it. Wasn't sure how to feel about that one, to be honest, but wasn't my decision to make. "Let the Patterson family do their thing, Fee. As long as we're safe and happy, why does it matter what they do?"

It mattered. I knew he understood that. Though I

did, for a moment, try to think about it in the terms he laid out. What if we did drop everything and focus on our own lives like everyone else in Reading seemed to? Was what the Pattersons wanted, whatever goals they set out for their family and our convoluted little town really all that important in the grand scheme of things? Even if it meant laws were being broken, people getting hurt…

Yeah, okay. Answered my own question. And from the second sigh Crew let out his mind had wound through the same process of thought and came to the same conclusion.

"You could have told me Dad made you an offer." I wasn't angry. The pair had been hanging out a lot together and I didn't exactly mind the fact they seemed to be close. After all, having my dad adore my future husband was a good thing, right? But secrets, still? "No more keeping things from me, please."

Crew sounded suitably contrite when he answered. "I was going to tell you," he said. "I swear. I just… I didn't know if it was what I wanted. I'm just tired, Fee." He paused long enough I worried the call was dropped before he went on again. "Talk to your dad before you make any decisions about backing Vivian. Okay? And I'll be home as soon as I can. Things are wrapping up here faster than I expected." That didn't sound like a good thing in his estimation, sorrow returning to his tone. "Go solve a murder, already, and leave the Patterson's pending disaster to another day. When I can be there to help."

"I love you." Why did my voice catch?

"Oh, Fee, sweetheart." He sounded so far away and yet right there, with me, words vibrating with sadness. "I don't know what I'd do if I didn't have you. I love you so much. I'll see you in a couple of days. Okay?"

I hung up after we said our goodbyes, heart heavy, wishing I could do something to ease the hurt he was living through, that he would just unburden himself on me already so I could feel useful instead of utterly useless on the other side of the country.

Nothing to be done about it right now. Instead of lingering over it, I could, instead, do as he asked and find out what happened to Melina Canty.

I drove, Liz next to me, pulling off the main road and down the new pavement toward the center as she spoke, mirrored sunglasses firmly in place, dark suit as familiar now as her shining ponytail.

"Forensics has cleared us to search Melina's office," she said. "I want to do a really thorough dig if you're up for it."

I nodded instantly, noting how different she was from Crew. He seemed to take a thorough approach with people while she was more about locations and situations. Probably why they had made a great team.

I wondered what she thought of my haphazard meanderings from interview to location to stumbling half steps into research. Though when I'd filled her in on what Charlie told me, she'd taken it in stride that he'd chosen to break into my apartment to talk to me.

Did stuff like that just not phase her? Meaning, did it happen to her often enough she didn't see it as odd? Gave me a modicum of comfort to think perhaps we were more alike than different.

As for Crew's treasure info reveal request, I'd held off. Not because I didn't trust Liz, but because it felt like he should tell her if that was what he wanted to do. And I'd support the choice whole-heartedly, as long as Daisy, Mom and Dad were on board. After all, this wasn't just my adventure to spill. There were more players in that little game these days.

Besides, I wasn't feeling particularly happy or excited or into the treasure hunt at the moment. Go figure.

As I pulled into the parking lot of the center, I took note of the familiar pickup truck and the tall, broad-shouldered figure leaning against it, his short, silvered hair catching the sunlight, button-up flannel shirt and jeans all Dad, all the time. I parked next to him and climbed out to hug him, though, for a brief and aching moment, I flashed out of that place and into memory—

Standing on a dock, dripping wet, Vivian's screams echoing across the water, Victor sinking into darkness and the shadow, always the shadow, looming over me before it ran away—

I blinked, coming out of my trance with my father's warm arms around me. I shook off the reaction to him, accepting his big, familiar embrace as he unwound from his casual waiting pose to welcome me.

Did he know I'd been gone a moment? If so, he didn't react that way, while my heart skipped, and I shoved off any possible belief my father had anything whatsoever to do with the death of Victor French.

Why, then, was I having these flashbacks to the boy's death at the weirdest moments? What was triggering my return to the past over and over again?

"Hey, kid," he said. "Hear congratulations are in order. That man of yours finally gave you what I couldn't." Dad poked at the badge hanging from my belt. "Looks good on you, Fee."

I swallowed hard, the emotion welling just another burden to bear. We'd talked about why Dad kept me from going to the academy, his attempt to protect me from the disappearance and supposed death of the woman they'd named me after, not to mention the influence of her father, local criminal mob boss Malcolm Murray. But it meant a lot knowing he understood just what he'd taken from me by denying me the career I was sure was my calling.

Dad didn't do anything lightly and I knew it hadn't been his intent to hurt me. Why then did grief linger over what could have been?

Regret could take a flying leap. Right along with his secretiveness.

"I hear you're trying to poach my fiancé into working for you." I poked Dad firmly in the ribs to hide my surge of feeling.

He grinned but there was a sheepishness to it that said he'd been waiting for Crew to tell me himself. "I have no idea what you're talking about." He winked. "And that would be working for us, Fee." Dad's eyes settled on Liz who cracked a grin in return. "Think any further about what we talked about, Agent Michaud?"

Liz laughed out loud while I gaped back and forth between them, amazed at my dad's audacity.

"Still thinking, John," she said, flashing me a rather guilty look though her amusement didn't fade. "It's a tempting offer. But the FBI kind of owns my soul at this point."

"Only if you let them," Dad said, firmly enough he actually meant it. "There's more to life than working for others, Liz, when you could be working toward something for you."

What was my father up to?

"I need to look in on Jimmy Hogan." Liz changed the subject so abruptly I struggled with confusion. "There's something about that kid that doesn't add up. After we tear Melina's office apart?"

"I want to talk to Gretchen first," I said. "If Charlie's suggestion pans out, maybe we can find what we need there."

"I'll leave you to it." Dad stretched, grinning. "Happy hunting, Deputy Fleming. Agent Michaud." He left, driving off while I watched him go, wondering if he'd come all this way to wait for us or if he had his own agenda.

Right. Who was I kidding? This was Dad I was pondering. Of course, he had an agenda. But why did it bring him here to the center?

Liz and I parted ways, her quick, strong strides carrying her toward the rider's apartments and mine to the main office. I didn't knock this time, didn't give the woman behind the desk time to argue. Instead, I gestured for Gretchen to stand, speaking quickly so she couldn't protest.

"I need a word," I said. "And to search your office."

Yup, argument pending. Except I flashed the badge on my hip and a glare that told her in no uncertain terms her ability to stonewall had run out with my patience.

Gretchen finally heaved a sigh and shrugged, angry if the frown lines between her eyes were any indication. "Fine," she snapped. "But I'm busy, Miss Fleming, and this continuing disruption is making it very hard for me to do my job."

"Nice of you to call Melina Canty's death a disruption." They'd been arguing. What about?

The facility manager looked suitably contrite. "I didn't mean it that way," she said, apologetic as she stood and circled her desk, standing in front of me with her arms crossed over her chest. "But you try telling the young riders who get one shot at the Olympic team that they are going to lose the chance they've spent their lives striving for because someone decided to kill Melina."

Hadn't thought of it that way. "What were you and Ms. Canty fighting about the day she died?"

Gretchen hesitated before dropping her hands, tossing them like this was a ridiculous thing to discuss. But at least she was talking.

"Melina didn't want Alphonse here," she said. "She's the reason he lost his job as the main coach." She hesitated like she was going to elaborate but instead changed her mind. "But he has the right to coach anyone he wants." Sounded defensive.

Hmmm. Didn't sound like the whole story. I circled her desk, looking around as I did. And took note of the large cabinet behind her chair. One of the drawers stood open and it was impossible to miss the contents.

Charlie had been right. The deep compartment was full of vials and syringes.

CHAPTER TWENTY

I turned slowly toward Gretchen, eyebrows arched, the obvious question aching to be asked. "May I ask why you need these particular items in your office, outside the clinic?"

She didn't seem concerned by the question, which made me second-guess my conclusion jump as she answered.

"I'm not just facility manager," she said. "I'm the main vet and consult with all of the riders and owners on equine health." I knew that. She'd told me she was Dr. Latrell when I'd attempted to question her. As if to reinforce her status, she pointed to a certificate over the cabinet where I did an unnecessary scan, reading the evidence of her status as a doctor of veterinary medicine. "Why?"

I shrugged off her question, quid pro quo. "What gauge needles do you usually use?"

Now she looked worried, curious but concerned. "Eighteen or twenty gauge depending on the viscosity of the injection." She didn't hesitate with that information. "Here. Let me show you." She crossed to me, looming over me, so much bigger than I was but not threatening so I didn't argue her move. She pulled open a second drawer below the first, revealing more boxes of syringes and sleeves of needles all in various sizes. "I keep meticulous records," she said, suddenly defensive all over again. "They are all accounted for, I assure you." Gretchen paused before her voice dropped in tone and volume, eyes big. "Does this have something to do with Melina's death?"

I didn't comment. "I'll need to see those records and then inventory your supplies."

She just nodded. I lost my confidence in her involvement at her innocent willingness to share. Not a hint of, "Talk to my lawyer," or any attempt to hide what she had. Either she was an excellent actress, or she had no idea Melina died from an injection.

"You have an alibi?" That question might have come out confidently, but it was half-hearted on my part. I didn't have an official time of death, but it was common knowledge by now the narrow window of minutes between Melina's argument with Sarah and my stumbling discovery of her body.

Gretchen reached for a clipboard and handed it to me. "I told Agent Michaud yesterday." She sounded sullen about it, as if only then realizing she wasn't supposed to be talking to me but, I guess, deciding it was too late so she might as well just carry on. "I was working with one of the horses. He's gone lame and we're trying to figure out if it's something serious or just a soft tissue injury."

It still felt like she was hiding something. Wishful thinking or truth? I wanted to dig deeper, just to be sure, be thorough. Now that I had license to do so, I found I had this annoying habit of wanting everything right now, please and thank you, don't make me come back and ask you again.

But when her phone rang, she used it as an excuse to cut me off, the sting of irritation I wasn't going to get to satisfy my growing hunger for answers zinging like a wound.

"My records and my supplies are at your disposal," she said, waving me out, closing the door behind me before answering the insistently wringing landline.

Was it the Pattersons calling her to task for speaking with me or was that just my paranoia mixed with the kind of narcissistic self-absorption that led me to believe the whole world revolved around me?

I headed out to join Liz at the rider's apartment complex, scowling at my feet as I exited the building. And almost missed the hissing argument going on between the two people who hastily shut up at the sight of me. I stopped in my tracks, Jimmy Hogan's discomfort obvious, though Violet Perry looked more annoyed by the interruption than guilty.

"Mr. Hogan," I said. "Did Agent Michaud find you?"

He looked startled, then nervous, shook his head. "I talked with Deputy Wagner yesterday," he said, one hand sliding through his dark hair. Wait, was that a dye line at his temple? Sheesh, poor kid, was he graying already? Sucked at his age. "What does the agent need?"

"Just some follow-up questions," I said. "Miss Perry, I had one for you. Apparently, the alibi you gave the deputy yesterday was false." I kept my tone flat and empty while the girl eye-rolled.

"Oh, for heaven's sake," she said while Jimmy glared at her like she'd done something horrendous. "I was with Charlie Chaswick, okay? You can ask him."

Confirming Charlie's story. "Why did you lie?"

She gave me a look that spoke volumes about her rapidly deteriorating character. "Honestly," she said, "he's nice enough to look at, but not good enough for me if you know what I mean."

Wow, classy.

"You're disgusting." Jimmy seemed truly offended while Violet tossed her long hair and shot him a glare.

"Grow up, Jimmy," she snapped before storming off, her boot heels thudding on the pavement.

He stared after her, face tight, shoulders hunched. "She doesn't deserve to be here," he said. "She treats the horses like they are objects, not living, breathing creatures. And that's a treat compared to how she talks to the rest of us." He met my eyes, the faint rims of the contact lenses he wore visible in the sunlight. "She's just a rich kid who rides for glory, doesn't care about our sport."

"What about Melina?" I knew Liz would be talking to him but took Jill's advice on the multiple questioner angle. "Did she care about her coach?"

Jimmy glanced around as if suddenly realizing he wasn't supposed to be talking to me before leaning in, earnest and serious. "Violet doesn't like anyone, as far as I know," he said. "But she's not smart enough or motivated enough to kill anyone. Too self-absorbed."

"And you, Mr. Hogan?" I dropped that on him casually, almost friendly in my tone. "Are you capable of murder?"

He flinched but didn't back down, though there was enough guilt behind his gaze I knew there was a lot he would rather I didn't find out. Which meant, of course, I would be digging. Liz had been right. He was hiding something.

"I didn't have anything against Melina," he said.

"And your alibi?" I waited while he floundered a moment.

"I don't have one," he said at last, head hanging. "I was with my horse. And he can't talk."

So, like Sarah Shard, his only corroborating witness was a giant, four-footed equine. Didn't bode well for him, especially if what he was hiding was motive for murder.

Liz appeared at my elbow, almost like magic, her

easy smile making Jimmy relax far more than mine had.

"Just who I wanted to see," she said. "Did you know I'm a rider, Mr. Hogan? I'd love to talk to you about your career. You know, to see if you can give me some pointers."

Jimmy's reaction was not what I expected. I figured he'd drop his defenses and loosen up. After all, that's what most people did when they were offered a chance to wax poetic about their passions. Instead, a giant wall of nope slammed up around him, expression going flat and hard, body tense.

"If you'll excuse me," he said, "unless you have questions for me about the case, I really have to be going."

Liz appeared as bemused as I was when Jimmy turned and practically fled from sight, leaving us both to stare after him in surprise.

"Well now," she said, sounding far too delighted by his retreat for it to mean any good for him, "I guess I know what to start digging into, don't I?"

His career? But what did Jimmy's riding record have to do with Melina's death?

Only one way to find out.

"Let's tackle his room again personally," she said. "I wasn't nearly as thorough the first time as I wanted to be. And no offense to your forensics people, but I have my own search standards I go by." She'd made that abundantly clear. "First," she said with a thoughtful expression, "I'm going to trust my gut. We have Melina's office to ransack and I'm thinking we might find something to help us figure out what to look for when it comes to the reticent Mr. Hogan."

If she said so. I was learning so much from Liz, such a nice shift from meandering my own instinctual way around investigating crimes. It was fascinating to watch her work, to track how her mind processed and made choices based on education and experience.

Crew might not have realized it, but he was on the verge of creating a monster and I wasn't about to let him know just how deeply I was falling into this new role I'd found myself filling.

As I followed Liz, though, I wondered if it was a natural thing for her or learned, this passion she had for police work. And why did the idea of tearing someone's stuff apart give Liz such a glow of happiness?

Better yet why was I grinning along with her?

CHAPTER TWENTY-ONE

It wasn't often I got to be on the opposing end of discovering someone snooping, so it was equal parts fascinatingly satisfying and alternately sheepishly embarrassing to walk in on Alphonse Brunbaugh with his hand in the cookie jar. If said receptacle of sweetness was Melina Canty's desk in her cordoned-off office.

Did I look that abjectly pathetic while stammering and stuttering over the reasons why I actually wasn't invading someone else's privacy? Surely not. I couldn't recall ever actually saying I was sorry or even attempting to hide my clandestine behavior. In fact, if anything, I typically had a slew of questions to ask whoever it was appeared to interrupt my nose poking, so we were nothing alike. Because

Alphonse, for his part, did a terrible job of attempting to cover up his sneaky behavior with clear guilt and only his own agenda written on his face.

"I was looking for something." He swallowed as he wrapped up his bumbling, stammer of a laughable shot at innocence with that particular gem neither Liz nor myself were buying. He had to know it, standing there all awkward and uncomfortable with the top drawer of the heavy wooden desk wide open and Melina's belongings spilling out over the surface where he'd summarily scooped and dumped in a haphazard manner akin to a child throwing a tantrum and their toys everywhere in some kind of Mommy protest.

And that was the big difference, wasn't it? When I snooped, I had the best interest of solving a crime in mind. This guy? Not an altruistic bone in his body, I'd venture. Yes, I admit, I was doing my best to make myself feel better and nailing it.

"I'm sure you were," Liz said, completely unaware of my internal conversation with myself, droll enough I couldn't stop the laugh that escaped. It was so tied into where my own thoughts had led me and I was already in the ballpark of justified behavior, so I guess I could be forgiven for my outburst. She didn't respond and I smothered it quickly but not fast enough to mask amusement or the lack of professionalism it denoted.

Damn, I had a lot to learn about being a cop.

And yet, my reaction seemed to have a good effect on Alphonse because he lost his utterly tense, deer-in-the-headlights of an oncoming freight train expression and settled into a more relaxed posture.

Liz observed all with her collected cool unruffled before speaking again. "But what you were looking for, Mr. Brunbaugh—that's the most interesting part."

I couldn't live through more stutters and attempts at lies. "Something incriminating, perhaps?" I hadn't meant to interrupt or cut into her interrogation but the awkward discomfort of his inability to lie effectively was too painful to watch. "A clue that might lead us to believe you wanted her dead?"

He flinched while I suddenly second-guessed speaking up after all. Had I just overstepped, interfered? No matter what I'd managed to uncover from my own poking and proddings in the past, Liz was the expert. And yet, I'd managed to get a lot of information from a vastly varied kind of people with very little effort over the years, so I had to trust my instincts.

As for Liz, she didn't seem put off by me speaking up. If anything, she seemed to lean into it mentally, as much as she did physically, her shoulder now resting against the door frame, arms crossing over her chest. Surely Alphonse didn't miss the fact when she did the front of her blazer opened, exposing her badge and gun? Wasn't lost on me. And there was no way Liz didn't realize such a physical stance produced that sort of view. Had maybe been taught how to look intimidating, or practiced it in front of a mirror? As a woman under 5'5", and petite, she had to be aware of her own lack of physical stature. And yet, from the bullies outside to this imposing man, Liz's subtlety seemed far more effective than the posturing I'd witnessed from the men she'd faced down.

Whatever the case, her simple act did the job. So, yeah. I was learning a *lot*.

"Nonsense." He tried for puffed-up self-importance and failed almost immediately, sagging once more despite his impressive height and rather broad shoulders. He was still in excellent shape for his age, at least mid-sixties if I had him pegged correctly, and I wondered about a man of his stature, the matching size of a horse big enough to carry him gracefully over jumps the height the riders here challenged regularly. Though I had to admit, I didn't know for sure he was a rider. Was that a thing? A coach who didn't ride?

Not likely. Not at this level. Now I was curious and distracted so it was a good thing Liz was there to pick up my wandering mind's slack.

Which she was happy to do, apparently. "We can do this all day," she said, "here or at the station. But we all know you're going to eventually tell us why you broke in here when it was clearly marked as off-limits. So just spill it and save all of us time and aggravation." She arched that perfect eyebrow at him. "Because trust me, Mr. Brunbaugh. Most of the aggravation will be yours."

He looked back and forth between us before sighing heavily, tossing his big hands and gesturing at the pile of papers, office supplies and rubber bands cluttering the surface of the desk.

"Melina and I had some... discourse." He licked his lips, tried to start again a couple of times before blurting on. "I sent her some correspondence and I wanted to get it back. Personal reasons."

"Hmmm," Liz said, meeting my eyes. "Threatening letter, you reckon?"

I nodded, taking her lead and running with it. "Probably telling her something to the effect of, 'if you do so and so or say such and such, I'll kill you'?"

Liz gave him a sideways look. "More than likely," she said. "Sounds plausible. And like motive."

Alphonse lurched around the side of the desk. Liz reacted immediately, her casual pose no longer so lackadaisical, whole body loose but clearly ready for anything, right hand pushing back the front of her blazer and fully exposing her sidearm.

"Careful, Mr. Brunbaugh," she said, voice low, deep, no longer teasing. "I'm going to ask you to stop right there and stay where you are until I've told you otherwise."

He froze in place, blinking and flushed, gaze flickering to her gun and back to her face before both hands leaped up, palms out and flat, shaking his head with his lips quivering.

"I'm sorry," he said. "I'm not threatening you, I swear. I just..." He seemed on the verge of an emotional outburst that had nothing to do with anger. "She was a horrible woman," he finally blurted, hands falling to his sides. "Just horrible.

Everyone hated her. This is terrible and just what she would have adored." He waved at the desk again, abstractly indicating toward whatever it was he'd been seeking. "To bring me down, make me a suspect in her murder, though I did nothing wrong. Nothing, I tell you."

"I'm sure if you're innocent, you'll be exonerated, sir," Liz said, relaxing somewhat. "Why don't you let us complete our own investigation and trust the law is on the side of those who have nothing to hide."

He looked ill, as if she'd told him to stick his head in the mouth of a gaping lion. "And if I'm falsely accused because of that letter?"

She shrugged. "Maybe you shouldn't be writing threatening letters then, sir."

Alphonse's wavering courage returned somewhat as she gestured for him to exit the room, stepping aside so he could pass through the doorway where he paused in the hall. "Did you look into Reis as I suggested?"

"We did," I said. "Tell me, did this letter of yours have anything to do with Ms. Canty wanting you off the property? Her attempt to keep you from coaching here?" Gretchen's suggestion there were those who wanted him out seemed to fit the bill.

"She was trying to have me banned," he huffed, then caught himself as if he'd spoken before he thought about what he was saying and to whom.

"Because?" I waited for the answer that never came.

"Perhaps you should just ask her." He bit those

words out in sharp staccato. "Or the person who murdered her."

Still didn't know it was murder. But yeah. It wasn't exactly a stretch to assume.

"Please don't leave town, Mr. Brunbaugh." Liz watched him carefully as she spoke. "We'll have more questions in light of this encounter. Especially once we read the contents of the letter. Have a nice day."

He was about to leave, my attention turning toward the office and my now eager need to dig into the contents of the desk. Who knew what other gems of juiciness lay contained inside? But he didn't get a chance, not when Gretchen Latrell came huffing down the hallway toward us.

I assumed she was going to lay into me and Liz. Instead, to my shock—and the agent's—the tall, broad-shouldered facility manager stuck a finger in Alphonse's chest, her own face a mask of fury.

"You bastard," she snarled. "I'll have you banned from coaching for this."

I would have loved to have known what the fight was about. But it erupted into a shouting match so loud and double-layered, I instead caught myself gaping in shock at the sudden, massive explosion of voices that echoed down the corridor. While feeling a surge of empathy for Crew, Jill, Liz.

Was it just me, just Reading? Or were people freaking crazy?

CHAPTER TWENTY-TWO

Liz let them argue a few moments, her head cocked as if trying to sort out what they were saying. Hoping to pick up something incriminating without interrupting the natural course of their fight? Clever, but only if they didn't mangle what they had to say with pitch and volume so aggressive the meaning got lost.

That was the truth in my case. I managed to register a few choice accusations, including botched competitions, inferior horses and something to do with Violet's seat, whatever that meant. Maybe Liz, more practiced at this sort of thing, managed to glean details from the mess of their screaming match, but if the growing frown on her face was any indicator, she wasn't enjoying the experience either.

Finally, clearly fed up and with her full-on authority showing in the set of her shoulders, the FBI agent at my side interjected with a piercing whistle produced by two fingers between her full lips.

Gretchen and Alphonse both fell instantly silent, though they glared at her like she had no right to interrupt before they realized they were doing so at a federal agent. Their expressions altered almost on cue to each other, rather comical if it hadn't been a murder investigation.

Supposed murder. Blah.

"You," Liz jabbed a finger at Alphonse, "lost your job as head coach here because of Ms. Canty. Correct?"

He nodded, sullen and closed off. "She fabricated lies about me," he said, inhaling in an obvious attempt to list said lies. Like we cared. Didn't.

Liz waved him off, pivoting toward Gretchen. "And you and Miss Canty had a falling out over her coaching practices at one point, I seem to recall."

The facility manager grimaced. "That wasn't public knowledge."

I hadn't heard that little tidbit, either. Was that what their fight had been about? Liz didn't make a big deal of it, shrugging. "People talk, Dr. Latrell," she said. "Especially if you speak their language. And as a fellow rider, I guess I qualify as trustworthy." I was not going to remind myself I'd spent the first part of this whole investigation being blocked by everyone I tried to talk to and refused to let bitterness about it seep in, especially against Liz. Still.

How much else had she uncovered because she didn't have a giant anti-Patterson sign hanging around her neck?

Right, because she had such an easy time as an agent getting people to talk. And wasn't trained and experienced and, like she said, tied to the showjumping world enough she used all her talent and skill to pull information out of those who didn't want to talk to her.

Sour grapes, Fleming.

Liz paused, squinting past the both of them as if thinking, though I was certain she knew exactly what she planned to say long before she said it and had this whole conversation firmly under control. "This is common practice, though, I'm aware of that. Riders switch coaches all the time."

It was? They did? News to me. But Alphonse was nodding.

"I didn't care I lost my position," he said, sniffing and elevating that wide nose of his, the snot. "I had no trouble finding a private coaching position and the flexibility and proper compensation my expertise provides."

"You get paid more as a private coach?" So, unless prestige was on the menu for motive, he had no reason to kill Melina. At least, over losing his job. But what other reason was there?

"I do indeed," he said. When Liz didn't argue I guessed he was telling the truth.

Gretchen, unhappy as she appeared, backed him up, too. "We paid you what you were worth,

Alphonse. The fact you convinced Sarah Shard's sponsors to cover your exorbitant fee is on them, not this facility."

But wait, didn't the Pattersons own the center? Sniff, sniff. Smelled less horsey and more fishy around here by the minute.

"Now, if you'll excuse me." Alphonse drew himself up like we'd offended him instead of caught him digging in an active investigation, "I have a rider to coach."

Gretchen frowned after him before beginning her pursuit and while perhaps I should have gone after them to try to overhear what was likely to be a continuation of their argument, Liz's hand on my arm held me back.

"I'm not convinced this whole job thing is the motive," she said, low and soft. "Considering riders switch out their coaches all the time... it's a competitive sport. And despite being an ass, a coach who's sent as many riders to the Olympics as Alphonse Brunbaugh has is in high demand." She shook her head. "So, if not, then who had reason to kill Melina Canty?"

My phone rang and I immediately answered it, putting Dr. Aberstock on speakerphone so Liz could hear what he had to say.

"Sorry to take so long," he said, sounding like his cheery self despite the apology. "The forensics lab is backed up. Some kind of issue in Perfection." The so-called "perfect American town" that had Olivia worked up since they'd started only recently trying to hijack her tourism slogan for their own uses? Two bergs over, it fell under the same jurisdiction. Before I could ask what was up, the doc went on. "Turns out you have a murder, not that you're surprised to hear it." He chuckled like he'd made a joke, not confirmed someone had killed someone else for reasons yet uncovered. "Let me see." The sound of papers rustling was followed by, "Ah, yes. Here we are. Melina Canty died from cardiac arrest brought on by a ketamine overdose."

"Ketamine?" Liz jumped on that right away while my brain tried to figure out where I'd heard that name before. "The tranquilizer?"

"Anesthetic, actually," Dr. Aberstock said. "That's a common misconception. Ketamine is used to sedate, not relax." Huh. "Whoever attacked Ms. Canty wasn't fooling around. The typical dose for a horse, according to the report, is 2.2 milligrams per kilogram of body weight. He grunted slightly. "Apologies for the metric." Greek. He was speaking Greek. But Liz was nodding so I didn't interrupt. "The dose in her body? Enough to put a 1000-pound horse to sleep."

"And enough to kill her, apparently." Liz was chewing her lower lip.

"Stopped her heart," he said. "Likely knocked her out within seconds before it suppressed her muscular ability to contract. Effectively suffocating her while inducing cardiac arrest."

Wait, I knew where I'd heard of ketamine before. "Isn't it a date rape drug?" Were we dealing with something much more insidious?

But the agent at my side, while agreeing with a nod, didn't look worried. "Tranks and sedatives are used in dosing horses," she said. "Most, if not all, are illegal in the showjumping circuit. Though why would you use something as strong as ketamine on a show horse? What kind of benefit would you get from knocking it out?"

Dr. Aberstock made a soft, unidentifiable sound. "No idea," he said. "That, my dear indomitable policewomen, is your job to figure out. Now, if you'll excuse me, I have other bodies who need my attention."

I hung up while Liz pulled out her own phone. She scanned what looked like a text message before looking up and meeting my eyes, hers tight with anger. It was so rare to see Liz mad—had I, even, ever?—I paid close attention when she spoke.

"According to my contact, there have been cases of sabotage, where horses who previously performed outstandingly have been showing behavioral issues in the ring to the point their riders and coaches are abandoning their rides because of danger to themselves and others."

"What does that have to do with ketamine?" I was about to do a search engine investigation when Liz beat me to it.

"Danton? My rider friend?" She pointed at the screen of her phone. "Guess what he says is one of the major side effects of sedation in a horse."

Seriously? "Behavioral issues?"

She nodded, grim, clearly upset. "Nervousness, manageability problems, focus and attention deficit." Liz put her phone away, face creased in a scowl. "You know, every time I think people can't lower their estimation in my eyes? They find ways to be even more disgusting." Her dark hair shimmered as she shook her head. "These animals are athletes, but they are innocent. They carry their riders out of love and their own passion for the sport. They've done nothing and yet, some asshat jerkoff is using drugs to hurt them." So, someone was a huge animal lover. Not that I wasn't. But whoa. "You'd better catch whoever it is who did this first, Fee," she snarled then. "Because if I do? I won't be held responsible for my actions."

Okay then. "How about we find the killer first," I said. "And then we can decide who gets to do what and in what order."

She growled something under her breath before nodding abruptly, right hand resting on the handle of her gun. I was very, very glad in that moment I wasn't the target of her upset. Because *day*-um.

Agent Michaud was *gangsta*.

"The question remains," I said as we turned and entered Melina's office, Liz closing the door behind us, "did the victim catch someone dosing a horse and was attacked and had the ketamine injected to shut her up?"

"Or," the agent said as she crossed to Melina's desk, "was she doing the doping and was caught in a struggle with a person who tried to stop her." She shrugged. "The end result is the same. But you're right about one thing. Knowing who was responsible might help us narrow down who to take a closer look at." She gestured at the desk. "Let's see if we can find some answers."

Liz appeared to have taken firm hold of her temper again. It felt oddly comforting to know she wasn't the perfect and all-powerful FBI agent I'd been building her up to be, despite knowing she was only human. On the other hand, seeing her temper told me more than ever we were kindred spirits.

I'd take it.

CHAPTER TWENTY-THREE

After a fruitless search of Melina's office (with no sign of the threatening correspondence Alphonse Brunbaugh had been seeking, unfortunately, so not even that to use against him), the fact we turned up zilch as to a connection between the coach and any kind of doping scandal, Liz next led me to the rider's quarters. I felt a brief tingle of guilt over the fact I'd been spending all this time on the case and none at all at Petunia's, leaving everything to Daisy, Mom and the staff, but when I texted my bestie to apologize while I followed Liz across the compound to the apartments, her reply made me grin.

All's quiet on the Petunia's front! She included a cute little pug emoji she'd downloaded onto our phones to share. *Have fun catching the murderer!*

That was Day in a nutshell. Nut being the operative part of the word. Though I had to admit as I put my phone away, she of all people knew just how much fun I had when there was a mystery to solve, so her wording wasn't exactly off-book.

So, if she was nuts, what did that make me?

Jimmy was nowhere to be found, likely working with his horse. Or disposing of evidence he'd killed Melina? Naw, if the kid was going to do that surely, he'd have done so right after the murder, right? Still, as I sifted through his life, knowing the techs had been over his room with their fine-tooth combing already, I wondered what motive he might have.

"Was she his coach?" I glanced at Liz who was studying a photo of Jimmy. She set down the wooden frame with a thump before frowning at me as if I'd interrupted and she was looking for an answer in her brilliant brain.

"I'm assuming you're referring to the victim and Mr. Hogan." Right, I had been pretty vague, but she'd sorted things out thanks to the context of our present location. "Yes, as far as I know. We can check, though. You're thinking what, exactly?"

"Nothing yet," I said, setting aside a small stack of golf shirts. We'd been here before, and I'd been forced to go through Jimmy's messy laundry already. I suppressed the need to sigh, to ask Liz what she hoped to find. Only to hear her expel air in a rush while she turned to me as if reading my mind.

"There's nothing here," she said. "I'm chasing ghosts, I think. But I can't shake the feeling, despite not having any evidence, Mr. Hogan is hiding something."

"I'm more than willing to trust your gut, Liz," I said. "Want to chase it down?"

She grinned. "I do," she said. "Thanks, Fee. You sound like Turner and that's what I need right now. The chance to chase the idea without the influence of these surroundings." She slipped free of her gloves, gesturing at the door. "After you, Deputy Fleming. I think your apartment fridge has a beer in it with my name on it."

That's how we found ourselves, about a half-hour later, perched on the stools in my private kitchen, sipping from chilled bottles and hunched over her notes. Early afternoon sunlight streamed in my widows, enough dust motes floating I realized I really needed to do a thorough cleaning of my apartment.

I will admit, within just a few minutes of attempting to review the case, we ended up talking about something much more personal.

"You're good for him." Liz started it, downing her first beer and half draining her second before she wandered off-topic. She squinted at me a long time, pointing with her index finger, the bottle in her hand balanced between her thumb and the rest of her digits. "Very good. I wasn't sure at first. Thought he lost his edge." She let the glass bottom thud to the countertop, faint regret on her face. "I'm sorry about that, Fee. He means a lot to me. We've been through so much together. I feel kind of…"

"Protective?" I didn't wait for her rueful nod.

"Me, too. I get it, Liz. Honest." And I did because I felt the same way.

"Don't ever tell him I said it," she laughed. "He'd be pissed at me. He's the one who likes to do the protecting."

"Tell me about it." I eye-rolled and laughed in turn. "Did he tell you how we met?"

Liz giggled, totally uncharacteristic. "He did," she said, eyes sparkling. "When you were kids."

Oops. Right. He remembered me, though I honestly had no recollection of him as a child when he and his father came to Reading to look for the treasure. Which made me think about the hoard and, oddly, have a flashback moment to something I wasn't expecting.

Standing on a dock, the dripping Vivian in my arms, screaming. And a shadow that I turned to look up at, a shadow who spun and ran away and let Victor drown—

I jerked out of the memory and took a shaking breath. Why did thinking about my childhood—and not remembering Crew's part in it—trigger that particular memory? The obvious answer tried to smother me in panic, but I shook it off. I'd already had this same instance surface, with Dad, right? Maybe being around men woke it up. Which told me the shadow was male…? Perhaps. But any thought at all that the shadowy figure had been Crew?

No way. Just no.

Liz was watching me with her FBI agent face. I waved off her quiet calm with a shaking breath. Before telling her about Vivian, Victor, that day. The shadow figure. And the recurring nightmare that plagued me, the memory that had only woken recently despite the fact everyone in town, it seemed, knew all about the fact I'd been there when Victor drowned.

Liz finished her beer before commenting, rising to go to the fridge to retrieve two more, returning with sodas instead, handing one to me which I accepted. We were on duty, after all. She sat again and spoke with a deeply thoughtful tone in her voice.

"Whoever let that boy die," she said, "it wasn't your fault, Fee. But that's what you're holding onto, isn't it?" I gulped, nodded. "You saved the girl instead of her brother and you feel guilty you had to choose."

I did. But Victor made me. Right? My memories from that day were so clouded by fear, by time's passage, but my own suppression of what happened. Could I even trust what I was recalling? If I, for instance, actually asked Vivian what she could tell me about the events of that day, what would she say?

And did I have the courage to broach the topic?

After all this time, did it matter who it was let Victor French drown?

"I can understand why you suppressed it," Liz said, softly, kind. "Honestly, I understand. There have been enough times I've asked myself if I could have done more, second-guessed my role in shootings, even though I knew—*knew*—I did everything by the book, the way I was supposed to." She sipped soda before going on. "Guilt sucks, Fee.

Not just because it's toxic, but because it can distort the truth to the point it makes us think we're in the wrong and just won't ever let us forget it." Liz tapped the side of her can with her fingers. "As long as we don't resort to unhealthy ways to hide from it, though, I figure we're winning." She set her drink down at last, leaning on her elbows. "I know enough agents and cops who've succumbed to their guilt I do my best to let it go. But for a little kid to have to carry that kind of burden?" Liz sat back at last, scrutiny uncomfortable because it was so compassionate. "You talked to Turner about it?"

I shook my head. "My parents, to a point." Why hadn't I mentioned it to Crew? Easy answer, the one Liz was just talking about. Guilt kept me from sharing, hadn't it? And, despite knowing better, the worry he might judge me for my failure. Perceived failure. Whatever.

"Tell him." She pushed the half-empty can of soda away with a grimace. "He deserves to have the chance to tell you it wasn't your fault."

I smiled, faint and a little fluttery with emotion, but planned to take her advice. "How'd you get so wise?"

Liz laughed then, running her hands over the thickness of her ponytail and tossing it back over the shoulder of her white dress shirt. "Is that what you call it?"

I shrugged. "I wish I was more like you." Whoops. Where did that come from? "Instead of running off half-cocked with my temper getting the best of me."

The agent's eyes narrowed, teeth working on the inside of her lip. "There are times I wished I was a redhead," she said. "That I just want to let my temper out. So there."

I thought about the box of hair dye in the trash at the stable and grinned. "Maybe we could give Crew a shock," I said. "Switch colors. Wonder what I'd look like as a brunette?"

Liz froze, stared at me, mouth hanging open. "What did you say?"

I fumbled over repeating the joke, but she was already reaching for her phone, tapping in her password, swearing softly under her breath while she searched for something. I watched in bemusement while her face twisted from frown to wide-eyed delight and the sharp, "Ah-ha!" that passed her lips was accompanied by a flash of her cell's screen.

A familiar face filled it, but one with blond hair, green eyes, as opposed to the brown-gazed brunette I was used to.

"We have to go back to the center," Liz said.

He looked nervous to see us, dropping the brush he used on his horse when Liz entered the stable. Jimmy patted the shoulder of the big gelding who shuffled his hooves in clear response to his rider's discomfort, soothing the creature back to quiet.

Did he know the agent uncovered his secret? He must have. The dejected expression on his face appeared almost immediately, even before Liz stopped with her hand sliding softly over the big horse's nose as she spoke.

"Hello, Jimmy," she said. "Or should I say, Edward Worth?" His head hung instantly. "I think it's time you tell us why you're pretending to be someone you're not."

We'd spent the drive in silence while Liz kept the details to herself and I fumed a bit. Felt like Dad and Crew all over again. Though, to be honest, she looked like she was having so much fun it would have been a shame to make her spill.

But as she identified the young rider as a fraud, I shed my disgruntled irritation. Right about the same moment Jimmy/Edward looked up—and bolted.

He threw the brush in Liz's face, spun and ran the other way. I'm not sure where he thought he was going to go. But running like that? Yup, sure made him look guilty of more than him being an imposter.

Liz chased him toward the back door while my instincts drove me sideways, into the nearest empty stall and through the big, gaping window into the yard. I ran for the back of the building, circling the end just as Jimmy came hurtling around it and crashed into him.

I wish I could say I took him down with my expert moves and physical prowess. But nope, all I succeeded in doing was slowing him to the point Liz caught up. As I toppled over backward from the impact with his slightly taller and heavier body, his hands shoving against my shoulders to aid in my fall, I collapsed into the manure pile while Jimmy tried to regain his momentum.

Liz leaped, landing on his back, sending him sprawling into the pile beside me. And while I was disgusted by the fact I was now sitting in a giant heap of horse dung, at least I wasn't face-first.

The agent pushed off, letting him rise just slightly, her knee in his back, cuffs coming out and rattling as she slapped them on his wrists.

"Mr. Edward Worth," she said, "you're under arrest for fraud and, quite possibly, the murder of Melina Canty."

CHAPTER TWENTY-FOUR

I sat next to the young man who slumped in the wooden chair across from Jill, Liz leaning against the deputy's desk with her arms crossed over her chest. I glanced anxiously at the reception area, spotting Rose on the phone, and knew Robert would be back at any moment if her pinched expression and hissing conversation told me anything.

Yeah, told me *everything.*

Jill didn't seem concerned by the nasty piece of work at the front desk playing tattle tale, however, as she conducted the interview that had Jimmy—sorry, Edward—nodding in dejected agreement.

"Agent Michaud is right," he said, lips thinned in what sounded like a mix of anger and bitter acceptance. "I'm Edward Worth." He made that sound like the worst burden in the world. What could make him not want to be himself? To hide who he really was?

"Mr. Worth," my deputy friend said, writing notes as her phone recorded the interview, "can you tell me why it is you've been lying about your identity?"

From Liz's expression, she already knew. Nice of her to keep me in the dark, grumble, mumble. I held that frustration in check as Jimmy/Edward shrugged, rubbing one upper arm with the opposite hand like a little boy caught being a very bad child and only sorry because he'd been cornered and forced to admit the truth. "Because I've been banned from the show circuit," he said, "and the only way I could ride was to try to hide who I really am."

Liz shifted her position, dropping her hands to the tops of her thighs, a faint trace of empathy on her face. Yup, she'd known all right. Didn't seem to judge him for it, though. "You had to know someone was going to figure it out." Liz didn't sound as if she was going to call him to task for lying. Nope, she seemed more sympathetic than I'd been expecting. Her statement still had him sighing.

"I thought I could get away with it." He looked up, met her eyes with his own brown ones. "It was worth the risk, you know?" Liz nodded while, still in the dark, I waited for him to go on. "I stayed out of the limelight, changed my hair, my eye color." He glanced at me, then. "You don't ride, do you?" I shook my head, bemused. "So, you don't get it. I wouldn't expect you to understand." He returned his attention to Liz who obviously did. "I was kicked out over five years ago and I've grown up a lot since then. Maybe I was kidding myself, but I had to try."

Liz's lips tightened. "It's not the same, is it? Riding less than the best."

His face twisted. He didn't answer, just hunched miserably with his eyes now downcast.

"Why were you banned?" Jill waited patiently, like she always did, for his answer while he hummed and hawed and seemed to ponder what exactly he was going to say before visibly giving up any attempt to gloss things over and squaring his shoulders at last.

"I cheated," he finally blurted. "Melina was my coach." He sounded like that hurt to admit, like he blamed her, even. "I was riding well, the best of my life. Then my horse got hurt." His lower lip caught between his teeth, voice shaking with emotion when he went on. "You're right, about riding horses of that quality. There's nothing like it. Not having that sort of athlete as your partner?" He shook his head. "I might as well have quit then and there. I didn't have any options, so I made a bad decision I've been paying for ever since." His hands clenched in his lap. "It was give him something to keep him in the game long enough to qualify or forfeit. So, I drugged him."

"And got caught." Liz was so matter-of-fact Jimmy/Edward seemed to take it like she was almost on his side.

"It wasn't my fault," he said. "It was Melina's idea. But as the rider, I'm responsible for my horse's drug test. That's the rule. She swore to me they wouldn't catch the dosing, that it was a one-time thing and I'd be fine. She was wrong." Bitter, yup.

"You realize that gives you an excellent motive for murder." I did my best to keep my own voice as low and level as Jill, as Liz and seemed to succeed because Jimmy/Edward kept talking.

"I chose the center because Alphonse Brunbaugh was head coach," he said. "I'd never ridden with him before, so I figured I could hide who I was." He tossed his hands before going back to that huddled, lost posture he'd worn since we'd sat him down. Part of me felt maternal, wanted to brush the bits of dirt and straw from his dark hair, the front of his shirt while I held myself tight and controlled against the itch in my fingers to stroke the bangs back from his forehead.

Seriously. My mommy instincts could shove it.

"But Alphonse lost his position," Liz said.

His heavy nod was filled with regret. "As soon as I realized Melina was taking his place, I knew my plan wasn't going to work. Likely wouldn't have anyway. I just…" he looked around at the three of us, imploring, hurting. "Horses are everything to me, showjumping my life. And I couldn't live with the fact I'd never be able to compete again after one stupid mistake."

I did feel sorry for him, wished there was something I could do. While accepting there was a good chance he killed Melina. Fitting end to the coach who killed his career, right? Though, where did he get his hands on ketamine? Did he steal it from Gretchen?

"I expected her to turn me in immediately," he said, misery so apparent I finally did reach out and pat his knee. Fee, get a grip already. But it served the interrogation well, because he turned to me then, tears in his eyes. "She was blackmailing me, making me do things for her."

"Things?" I asked the question kindly, mind racing over possibilities.

He hesitated then spoke. "She had me doping other riders' horses. Sneaking into the stalls at night and giving them mild doses of anesthesia so they'd have performance issues the next day."

Wasn't that one of the side effects of ketamine? That meant he had access to the drug and the syringes. Another bump up for him on the suspect list.

"Mr. Worth," Jill said, "you do realize you're the one with the history of drugging your horse. Melina Canty's record is clean. So, it sounds very much like you're blaming someone who has no history of wrongdoing for something you've been proven to have done. And now you've given us excellent reason to believe you have a motive for her murder."

He twitched, eyes huge. "Wait, no, that's not right. I didn't kill her, I swear it." He turned to me again. Did Jimmy/Edward see me as an ally? I wasn't going to disabuse him of that notion if it meant we got more information from him. "But I do have proof she was guilty of doping." I nodded to encourage him to go on. "I know where she hid her stash."

"Where were you when Melina was killed, Jimmy?" Let him believe I cared. I was okay with that because I kind of did. Neither of my fellow officers complained about the rapport I'd created with my mothering, so I let the young man beside me answer with only the barest amount of guilt.

"Breaking into Melina's office," he said, barely above a whisper. "Looking for something, anything, to stop her from blackmailing me. I'd decided to leave, go home. Quit riding. I just wanted out. But she was going to have me arrested. That is until I found where she was keeping the drugs she gave me to dope the horses." He sat up a bit straighter. "I erased the footage, but I kept a copy." Learned that from Charlie, did he? "I can share it with you." He hesitated then rushed on. "There's a false bottom on the last, lowest drawer of her desk. Press the keyhole and it releases a little hatch." Good to know. "I was going to turn it over to Gretchen, I swear. And then go home."

Robert had the sort of timing that irritation is made of, storming into the office just as Jimmy was wrapping up. He joined us in a stomping huff, a bit out of breath as if he'd hustled for the first time in his life to get to us, glaring around at the three of us like we'd purposely cut him out. Well, we had, I guess, except we were just doing our jobs, weren't we?

Before he could make a further idiot of himself,

Jill spoke.

"Mr. Worth, we have to confirm your statement, but I'm going to hold you for now while we investigate what you told us. Do you understand?"

Jimmy/Edward didn't argue. Jill met my eyes for a second, a slight widening and then a flickered glance toward the door telling me what I needed to know. I slipped out while she let Robert manhandle the kid into the first cell, Liz ducking out behind me.

It was a fast, quiet ride to the center, a rapid speed walk race to Melina's office. I beat Liz just by half a step, but she grinned and let me go first, handing me a glove that slid over my hand while I sat swiftly in the dead coach's chair. I pressed the lock on the lower drawer as instructed and heard the satisfying click, sliding the whole mess open to find the hatch had released, as promised. Whistling softly while Liz took a photo.

Jimmy hadn't lied. The false bottom was lined with syringes and small vials. I lifted one out, turned the label into the light and exhaled a breath I felt like I'd been holding since the young, banned rider told us about this hiding place.

"Ketamine," Liz said out loud.

But did this mean Jimmy/Edward was our murderer or that someone else got to Melina Canty first? Someone who knew what she was up to?

CHAPTER TWENTY-FIVE

Dr. Aberstock's gloved hands neatly tucked the evidence away inside a box he then slid into a large plastic bag, the seal strip pulled away with practiced efficiency while we spoke.

"This could very well be the source of the ketamine," he said, keeping his voice low. We were still alone, at least for now. He'd been my first call when I'd discovered Jimmy/Edward's instructions paid off and the doc had arrived in short order with what he needed to bag and tag the evidence. I realized as he did so I should have called the forensics lab, but Dr. Aberstock didn't seem to mind nor find it odd he was my go-to, so I didn't apologize for dragging him away from the morgue to establish chain of custody for the syringes and vials. "But I won't know until the lab tests this particular batch and matches it—or doesn't—against the remains in the syringe you found." He examined one of the plastic syringes through the evidence bag, squinting at the brand name on the thin sleeve housing it. "Not sure if the brand is a match, Fee."

All good for now. "So, let's suppose she was on her way somewhere to dope one of the horses." I needed to find out whose horse was close to where she'd been found, who her target might have been. "And encountered someone who either had a beef with what she was doing or was fighting with her for another reason." The doc nodded as he wrote on the surface of the bag with a big black marker. He might not have been Crew or Jill or Liz—or even my dad— but Dr. Aberstock had been at enough crime scenes I was sure he could handle a talk-through of the crime and maybe even offer a new perspective. "They fight and a struggle ensues."

He looked up at me over the rim of his glasses, pausing in his notation on the bag. "I did discover evidence of bruising on her right wrist. And, from the small callous on her right middle finger near the nail, she wrote with her right hand."

Good to know. "So, a struggle." I let it unfold in my head, seeing the action, practically smelling the stable, the dimness of the interior of the walkway, the dust floating in the air, the fight as the victim fought off her attacker. "The murderer gained control of the syringe, already loaded to inject the horse." My hand rose and fell, the side of my fist hitting my thigh where the puncture mark had shown on Melina's body, left side. "Crime of opportunity." I depressed the imaginary plunger with my thumb while Dr. Aberstock watched, faint smile on his face. I tilted my head at him, thinking about body positioning. "Would be awkward to stab someone you're facing. At least in that location."

He nodded again. "There was additional bruising around the victim's neck," he said, "and collarbone."

"As if she'd been grabbed from behind, maybe?" I shifted the image in my mind around until a taller, stronger someone was holding her and grabbed the syringe, driving the needle into her leg. "That makes sense."

"And means if I can venture my opinion," the doc said, "whoever killed her was left-handed."

Ah! "Totes, doc," I said with a grin. "Awesome."

He beamed at me, tucking the marker, his gloves and the evidence bag away into his carry case. "Nice to be on the crime-solving side, for once, instead of being just an evidence gatherer." Like he was just anything. "How fascinating."

We left together, the doc heading off to the hospital while I headed for the stable and the scene of the crime. I'd barely made it around the corner when I caught Charlie peeking out, watching me, and knew then he'd been spying on me and the doctor in Melina's office. He ducked out of the way, but I was faster, circling the stable to the side door and catching him as he tried to escape that way, almost running into him though I was expecting his attempt to flee.

He came to a halt at the sight of me, looking both ways like he wanted to run before sighing and shrugging, hands spread in front of him in surrender. "Just curious," he said.

"Likely story," I said. And had a thought as I reached for the pitchfork next to the door and tossed it toward him.

What do you know? He caught it with his left hand.

"We need to talk, Mr. Chaswick," I said. "Now."

He glared a moment before setting the fork aside and grabbing my hand, dragging me into one of the empty stalls. Suddenly nervous, I felt myself tense at the proximity, his anger and upset so clear I wished again Jill had let me have a gun.

"I know you're just doing your job," he hissed in my face, "but you're going to ruin my cover if you keep this up. And I can't afford that. Do you understand?"

His cover? "I don't," I snapped back, "but if you have something I need to know, you can be sure I'm not going to stop digging until you tell me."

Charlie's expression settled into resigned frustration. "Fine," he whispered this time, "listen closely and pay attention, Deputy Fleming, because I'm not going to say it again." He glanced out into the walkway before tucking his lips against my ear and speaking before I could retreat in shock at the closeness. "I'm DEA."

Drug enforcement? "What are you doing here?" I

stared up at him in shock while his lips thinned, and he took one more look outside. He froze as he did, then sagged with a hint of relief, so when Sarah slipped into the stall next to me, I realized she was in on whatever it was he was working on.

Relief because I now knew Pamela's niece had to be innocent. Right?

"I was assigned to keep an eye on Melina Canty," Charlie said while Sarah watched with a pinched expression and her own nervousness. "And Sarah is my insider. She got me this job, said I'd worked with her at her old facility." Sarah was nodding, biting her lower lip.

"After my last competition," she whispered, "one I lost when I was favored to win. I wasn't part of the drug testing cycle, but I had my horse checked out anyway, for my own peace of mind. He was acting totally out of character, upset, misbehaving. The test came back positive for ketamine." She glanced at Charlie who was keeping an eye out past the door of the stall, so she went on as if his silence was approval for her to continue. "Charlie approached me, the DEA. They knew about the test, had been monitoring the issue. Not because of horse doping, though."

Charlie's turn. "A large amount of ketamine was stolen from a clinic in Connecticut," he said. "We were concerned since it's often used as a date rape drug, so we've been tracking that particular batch. When Sarah's test was flagged, I was sent to look into it." His lips twisted in a wry grin that had zero humor in it. "Imagine our surprise when we found out the drugs that were stolen were being used to sedate and influence horses in showjumping."

"Still a terrible use," Sarah snapped.

Charlie shrugged. "Agreed, which is why I lingered." He met my eyes, his serious. "I meant what I said about Gretchen. I'm positive she's in on this and likely killed Melina over the doping. Either she knows—I'd be shocked if she didn't—and wanted Melina to stop or the two of them fought over something else I haven't discovered yet."

"I'm positive Gretchen knows," Sarah said, grim and angry. "She's a vet, Fee. She knows what the side effects of mild anesthesia looks like. And it's been happening enough she had to have made the connection." Anger flared. "Melina died next to SuSu's stall. You know what that means?" She looked like she was about to blow a gasket, cheeks dark red, eyes wide and furious. "Melina or Gretchen were likely planning on dosing her. *SuSu*." Sarah's jaw worked, hands clenched at her sides. "I didn't kill her, but if I'd caught her doing that to such an amazing horse…" she exhaled heavily, seemed to pull her temper under control. "Charlie's been working for the DEA all along, but I've been working for the Olympic committee. They want answers and to uncover the perpetrators. It's been happening far too often. I'd come to the realization Melina had to be the one supplying the product, but I still have no idea how she gets it."

"Not Gretchen?" Couldn't she just order it? But

no, wait. The stolen batch.

"No proof of that," Charlie said, teeth gritted. "That's why no arrests have been made." His eyes narrowed, hands fisted. "I'm after a bigger fish, the source of the stolen ketamine. Melina's death couldn't have complicated my job more."

"Or it could reveal who the thief is," I said. "We could have been working together all along, you two."

Charlie looked unrepentant but Sarah grasped my hand and squeezed before letting go, like a physical expression of her regret.

"Just keep me posted if you uncover anything," I said. "I'll say out of your way if you stay out of mine."

Sarah nodded, glancing at Charlie for his agreement, which he gave with a curt nod before leaving the stall abruptly, slipping away. Sarah, on the other hand, lingered, her worried expression deepening.

"Fee," she said, "have you seen Aunt Pam?"

I wasn't expecting her to change the subject. She caught me flat-footed, and I shook my head with a frown.

"I haven't," I said. "Not since the other day when she asked me to help you."

She inhaled sharply, eyes widening. "I can't reach her," she said, tears in her eyes. "I think something might have happened."

While I was usually the conclusion jumping type, and despite the fact my heart clenched in response to her fear, I shook my head and did my best to act natural.

"I'm sure she's fine," I lied as my gut went cold and I fought off the urge to blurt out my own worry. "The Patterson weirdness is making it hard to get to her, that's all."

Sarah accepted my explanation, likely because she wanted to. I let her go, slipping out of the stall myself a minute after she departed to give us time to go our separate ways.

A whole minute I spent anxiously gnawing my thumb and glaring at nothing while the fear something had happened to Pamela grew and grew.

CHAPTER TWENTY-SIX

I went home to Petunia's, checking in with the desk before heading for the kitchen where I was greeted by my grinning, snorting pug who checked out the smell on my sneakers just prior to sitting at my feet like she expected me to fill her in on my day.

Mom looked up from the cupcakes she was decorating, a white pastry bag filled with chocolate icing oozing a bit of sugary goodness out the silver tip and I joined her, surprised and, then again, kind of not to find Liz, Dad and Jill all hovering around the tray of confections.

Was it the case that brought them together or the smell of Mom's baking? I was fifty-fifty on the reason because the heavenly scent of my mother making cupcakes could resurrect the dead. Ahem. No pun intended.

I helped myself to a cupcake, peeling it with a grin while the other three joined me as if they'd been waiting for someone to make a theft to justify their own snatch and grab. Considering I knew from experience my amazing mother would tolerate a sample—she wouldn't have been doing her decorating out in the open if she didn't figure, nay, expect us to help ourselves—I wasn't exactly taking my life into my own hands.

Wow. Since when did I start to think of my existence in terms of murder? Um, since I started finding dead bodies all over the place, obviously.

Mom didn't comment or even sigh as I knew she wouldn't, just went back to icing in slow, practiced circles of chocolatey goodness as if we hadn't depleted her stock of yummy fantastic by four fat cakes.

I filled my fellow officers in on what I'd discovered, from the confirmation of the drugs in Melina's drawer to the reveal that Charlie was DEA and Sarah herself working for the Olympic committee.

Dad grunted as he brushed crumbs from the front of his plaid shirt, a waste that Petunia was eager and delighted to clean up for him as the bits hit the floor. "I've been tracking Edward Worth for a week now," he said. Shrugged at me with a grin when I scowled in response. Nice of him to let me know. "What? I was working a case for a different branch of the Olympic committee." Another tidbit he'd failed to share. Not really out of character for John Fleming, Mr. Closemouthed Secretpants, but there you go. Still annoyed by the omission. "They suspected his real identity, and I was confirming for them before they had him evicted from the center." His eyes narrowed as he grabbed another cupcake, Mom's pointed stare a warning. We got one. That much I never doubted. Two was pushing it. Like, if she actually caught you, there might be regret involved before you got to eat it. Of course, Dad got away with more than most because Dad. I hoped, however, to avoid the unpleasantness that could arise if he decided to really shove luck to the edge of a cliff and see what happened. Because three? Meant bloodshed, tears and epically proportioned guilt that could bring down a small government.

Dad just winked at her and went on as he peeled the paper wrapper from the bottom of the perfect, moist delicious that was his prize for all those years being married to Mom.

Maybe it was worth risking taking another.

Dad went on around a mouthful like he was fearless, and the razor's blade of danger was his bread and butter. "I didn't know about Charlie Chaswick and Sarah Shard, however," he said. "Must be losing my edge."

Liz, meanwhile, was sampling the icing on the top of her first cupcake with her index finger while reading a text on her phone. "Confirmed," she said. "My friend Nick at the DEA says Charlie's been working the ketamine case, so his story checks."

"That leaves us with a shortlist of suspects," Jill said, all efficiency as she flipped open the cover of her notebook and reviewed the tidy handwriting. "Violet Perry."

"She's just a spoiled brat," Liz said, nibbling her cake. She looked around at us, lips twisting. "I've seen her type a million times before," she said. "Daddy's money, riding the best horses but treating them like crap because she just cares about winning."

"If her horse was doped?" I know she had to have thought through the idea herself. "Would she be angry enough about losing to kill Melina?"

"Maybe," Liz said, munching thoughtfully. "It's a tough sport, Fee, especially at this level. But would she get her hands dirty?" She set aside her own wrapper, dusting her hands over the counter to shed the loose crumbs. "Doubtful."

"And," I offered, "Dr. Aberstock said there was bruising around Melina's collarbone. Violet is tiny. Too small to be able to hold the taller woman that way."

"Unless she was on her knees," Jill suggested. "But she has a solid alibi if she was with the DEA agent."

Right. Charlie. "So Violet is out," I said. "Next?"

Jill looked apologetic but said the name anyway. "Sarah Shard."

Fair enough. "I think we've established she's got a temper," Dad said. "And she's tall, tall enough to have left the bruising the doc mentioned." Agreed, if grudgingly. "She suspected Melina already, thanks to her horse's performance. And the committee hired her to spy on the victim. So, it's possible."

"Except," I said, thinking about Sarah and her touch earlier, how she'd reached for my hand with her right one, "she's not left-handed."

Dad nodded then. "Let's file her away for the moment. Who's up?"

Jill consulted her notes. "Alphonse Brunbaugh."

"No motive that we know of," Liz said. "Though if he's known Melina this long, maybe he knew about the doping? Retaliation for going after his riders—at least, their horses?"

Possibly. "We don't have proof of that." Though he did have a grudge against her. "Doesn't he have an alibi?"

Jill nodded. "He was caught on camera sneaking into Melina's office around the TOD." Likely looking for that damned letter. Still, her office was close enough to the stable where her body was discovered… could he have killed her and then scooted over to dig through her stuff? Then again, everything was close by, so without a solid time of death—the window Dr. Aberstock gave us was a half-hour so not much help—anyone, even those with alibis, could have done it.

Not helping.

"I'll look into him further through my contacts," Liz said. "Who else we got?"

"Jimmy Hogan," Jill said. "Sorry, Edward Worth." She lowered her notebook and frowned. "He's on camera, too, also at Melina's office." Jill pulled out her phone and showed us the video he'd shared with her. In the running image, Jimmy crept into the space, dug around in her desk a second then perked. He ducked out the window just before the door eased open and Alphonse appeared.

I leaned away from her screen and shrugged. "What about Emile Reis?"

Dad shook his head. "He's clean," he said. "He was on a conference call the whole time." Liz arched an eyebrow at my father. "What? I looked into the guy. Sue me."

She laughed. "Flemings," was all she said.

I took that as a compliment.

"And Gretchen Latrell?" I prompted Jill who nodded. But it was Liz who spoke again.

"I like her for it," the FBI agent said. "She's a vet, knew the side effects. This facility and the horses are her responsibility. If she found out the coach she trusted was doping, she could have lost it." Liz shrugged. "I know I would have."

"That is if she wasn't in on it," Dad said. "I'm not convinced she wasn't."

Liz looked suddenly uncomfortable. "I know," she said. "I get it. I just hate animal cases." She shuddered. "Give me a nice, clean murder of someone who earned it. Kids and critters? Gets my blood boiling."

Dad looked like he agreed.

Jill's phone rang and she answered it on speaker. "Go ahead, Dr. Aberstock."

"I take it you're not alone?" He must have picked

up on the fact he was being broadcast.

"Fee, John and Liz are with me," the deputy said.

"Excellent." The doc's usual chipper nature shone through. "I can now confirm the syringe Fee discovered in the manure pile does not match the brand that Melina Canty had hidden in her desk." He hesitated before speaking again. "Apologies for getting your hopes up at the scene, Fee."

Wait, what? "How is that possible?"

"I'm sorry to be the bearer of complications," he said. Did he seem a bit downbeat about that? If so, he hid it well as he went on. "However, the syringe in question did contain the same chemical composition from the batch of ketamine recovered." He paused a second before speaking again. "I tested it myself, knowing how slow the lab is. Haven't lost my skills with a chemistry set, apparently." He sounded pleased with himself. "Honestly, it wasn't hard to match them. The ketamine from the syringe and the doses in Melina's desk contained a tracking tracer element left there by the manufacturer. I just had to look for it and voila."

"So, not her syringe," Dad said slowly, processing, "but her drugs?"

"That is how things appear at the moment," Dr. Aberstock said, far too cheery for the news he'd delivered. "I might suggest looking into the facility's vet. According to a purchase order I managed to dig up, she's a frequent buyer of the brand in question."

"Which means," my mother spoke up, all of us staring at her, Dr. Aberstock equally silent, while the neatly aproned vision of loveliness went on, "Gretchen and Melina were working together."

Liz shook her head, though not in denial, while Jill stood, nodding to Mom who silently handed the deputy a cupcake, then the FBI agent before slapping Dad's thieving fingers from taking a third.

"Looks like you three have an arrest to make," my mother said, licking icing from her knuckle.

CHAPTER TWENTY-SEVEN

Gretchen didn't seem nearly as surprised to see us as she would have if she'd been innocent. How telling was that? Heaps, in my books. Instead of arrogant disdain or even outright shock we'd returned, she stood slowly, as though a great weight rested on her shoulders and she struggled against it. She stopped when finally upright, watching from behind her desk while Jill grimly nodded.

"Dr. Latrell," she said, "you know why we're here?"

The facility manager just sighed, as much a proclamation of guilt as any sound I'd ever heard. "I admit it," she said, suddenly appearing harried and tired. Keeping a murder a secret was a giant load to bear, I guess. "I knew you'd catch me eventually. So yes, I know why you're here."

Wow, that was easy. "You admit to murdering Melina Canty?" I usually had to push the guilty into almost killing me in turn before they confessed. Maybe this cop thing was to my benefit after all.

Yeah, nope. I gave her too much credit too soon. If the confused and then horrified look on Gretchen's face was any indication, she wasn't giving up the whole truth and nothing but the truth so help me, ma'am, just yet. "No!" She shook her head while Jill pulled out her cuffs, the rattling sound always unnerving to me. "I didn't kill Melina. I was working with her."

Ah. So that's what she'd been admitting to. "You were drugging horses?" How horrendous. Here I'd thought maybe she was defending them. But a veterinarian treating animals like commodities to be used against riders for sport? Surely there was some kind of do no harm tenet in her kind of medicine like there was in human practice?

Well, there were doctors out there who cared little for patients of the two-legged variety so it did make sense there'd be bad seeds on the four-legged end.

Liz's disgust was impossible to hide. "You're a disgrace to the sport," she snarled.

Gretchen's head hung, no argument forthcoming. "It started small," she said, tone weary, worn. "An additive here, an anti-inflammatory there. Melina caught me at it. I was trying to help." She seemed to be pleading with Liz to understand. "These riders, they insist on the best performance from their horses. But they abuse them, treat them like machines, not the living creatures they are."

"Oh, and giving them sedation to enhance behavior issues isn't abuse?" The FBI agent's disdain cut the air with her sharp response. "Spare me your excuses."

"I didn't start out to interfere with the sport," Gretchen said, hands spread wide in supplication, looking for someone to see her side while we all just waited for her to tie the last loop in the noose and hang herself. "Just to ease pain for suffering animals riders insisted on using despite injuries. But when Melina caught me… she started blackmailing me into helping her."

More motive. And a pattern for Melina. She'd been doing the same to Jimmy. Had the two worked together, perhaps? To eliminate the woman who'd been holding their bad deeds against them? "She was influencing competition by interfering with performance."

Gretchen nodded, clearly miserable. "I continued to deliver what help I could," she said. "Melina supplied the drugs, variations I'd never heard of before, types that labs didn't know to test for." She pulled open the drawer of her desk while Jill and Liz tensed, pausing a moment with a surprised look on her face that they both now had their hands on their sidearms. I counted myself lucky I didn't share their immediate instinct the woman in front of us was reaching for a weapon, though I had no doubt it was their training that kept them alive.

Still. If living on a hair-trigger was the result of being a cop, maybe I didn't want a full-time part in it.

Gretchen slowed down, slipping a keyring and a single silver key from the opening before handing it to Jill. The deputy accepted it, eyebrow raised.

"There's a refrigerated lockbox hidden under the spare tire in my SUV," the facility manager said. "It's wired into the back via the USB power hookup. You'll find the drugs I use in there."

Modern tech. So convenient.

"And the ketamine you used to kill Melina?" Liz prompted with her next question. "Your syringe, her drug?"

But this time Gretchen shook her head, adamant. "I didn't kill her," she said. "I gave her a box of my syringes because she didn't have the size she needed. But that's it, I swear."

Hmmm. Despite the frowns on my friend's faces that said they disagreed I was starting to wonder if Gretchen might have been telling the truth. Why admit to the doping but not the murder?

Because murder had a giant penalty, I guess.

Jill wasn't doubtful, circling the rest of the way with her cuffs held out. "Turn around, please, Dr. Latrell."

Gretchen did as she was told after a long, agonizing moment. I watched her face contort, the panic rise and ebb from her eyes. Jill firmly and confidently slipped the silver bands around her wrists when she finally put her back to the deputy, reciting

Miranda rights as she led the vet and manager out of the room. She paused only long enough to hand me the key to the woman's SUV which I accepted.

Liz went with them, but I lingered, carefully going through all of Gretchen's things, from her desk to her cabinets and the drugs therein. I even took a trip to the small vet office on the property, finding Gretchen's black SUV with the equestrian center logo on the side, parked out front. I did a quick look around her little clinic before doing my due diligence and photographing the fridge unit box that was exactly where she said we'd find it, under the big, heavy spare in the back of her vehicle.

Surprisingly, there wasn't an ounce of ketamine to be found. Not even in the clinic, though when I internet searched a few of the labels I found other kinds of sedatives. So, she didn't stock ketamine, used alternatives instead. On purpose?

A text set my phone humming and I checked it quickly as I closed down the back hatch of the SUV. Dr. Aberstock's message was quick and clear.

Further bruising surfaced. Estimated height of attacker at least six inches taller than the victim. And miscalculation on the stab trajectory. Closer analysis suggests frontal assault. Means attacker is right-handed. Collarbone bruises from arm across the neck in front, not grasped from behind in that case. Apologies for the confusion. He included a little diagram he'd clearly drawn and photographed, showing body positions. How Melina faced her attacker, the taller murderer stabbing downward and to the side, forearm pressed to her throat. Another ding and a further image showed the bruising had fully formed around the puncture, that the damage had spread downward, confirming the needle didn't go right in but on an angle toward the ground.

I noted he'd forwarded the text to all three of us—actually four, because Dad's number was on the list. I pondered the information as I did my own version of his text, sending the photos of the box to Jill with a request to have the forensic techs come get it, along with my research into the fact Gretchen used other sedatives.

I could have gone to the sheriff's office and watched the two officers I admired interrogate their suspect, but I was suddenly tired. They didn't need me anymore. I noted the memory of Gretchen handing the key to Jill with her right hand and shrugged. The left-hander theory had eliminated more doubt.

Instead, I headed home. Petunia followed me around as I made myself busy, catching up on some tasks I'd meant to finish but hadn't had time to tackle thanks to the case. After the early evening ordering supplies and fixing a leaky toilet, I retreated to my apartment for a few minutes to sit and put my feet up, noting my computer was open.

I wiggled the mouse and realized, with a start of surprise, Liz had been using my laptop. And failed to log out of the FBI database.

The temptation was far too much. I don't know why I did it, only that I knew I'd likely never get another chance. And while digging around was as immoral as it was illegal, I couldn't help myself.

The Pattersons.

Blackstone.

Peggy Munroe.

Fiona Doyle.

It was an interesting and yet unenlightening trip down a path I'd already walked. At least, as I sighed and sat back a half-hour later, I wasn't being kept in the dark. I knew what the FBI knew about every topic that had my attention. I thought about Victor French, about the treasure hoard, but figured I'd pushed my luck as things were. I logged out a little regretfully, though knowing I'd done enough to satisfy my curiosity without, hopefully, making a mess.

One last internet search crossed my mind as I planned to get up. Just a nudge, a whisper of a question considering. Didn't Liz say it was a small community, that everyone in the sport at this level knew each other?

The moment I hit enter on my query, a photo popped up and I knew. In my heart, I knew.

Gretchen was innocent. And I had ID'd the killer.

CHAPTER TWENTY-EIGHT

Of course, I called Liz. Jill. Dad. No one was answering. Seriously? At a time like this? Where were they? Well, Liz and Jill were interrogating Gretchen, fair enough. But my father? Surely, he'd be available.

Yeah. Nope. Sigh.

I found myself in my car, driving toward the center before I could stop myself from making a terrible decision. But I promised myself, as I climbed out of the driver's seat and slammed the door, hurrying in through the gates and toward the main building, I would only identify the proof I needed and then skedaddle, doing nothing to alert the murderer to the fact they'd been figured out.

No way was I interested in being a target for another life-threatening attack. But if I didn't hurry, it was very possible the evidence I needed would disappear forever.

He didn't have an office of his own anymore, but he did drive a fancy SUV. While it was locked tight, I knew where to find the keys. A glance at the paddock told me I had the time I needed to find the means to break into his vehicle, so I took it.

Forensics had searched his room, so I knew he wouldn't have hidden anything there. But Gretchen's hiding place? Melina suggested it to her, hadn't she? Which meant it was a learned behavior. Learned from the very person she'd trained with herself when she was an Olympic hopeful. The image of them together, in a newspaper article, of her standing next to him, her horse between them, was a fraud, a sham, pretend happier days, though for all I knew Melina had been happy under his tutelage once.

His keys weren't out in the open but right where I expected to find them, in the pocket of a jacket tucked in his closet. I helped myself, exiting the building and heading back to the parking outside the apartment complex. Funny how the building that housed the riders and coaches looked exactly like the ones where the horses lived. I didn't bother contemplating the implications of that—who was more important, then?—and instead helped myself to the back of his SUV.

And the evidence I needed to convict him of murder.

Except there was nothing. No fridge box, no USB connection to a clandestine hiding place for ketamine or syringes. Nada, zippo and, in that moment of realization, my heart fell.

I'd been so sure. Alphonse and Melina, their photo from their glory days. They'd been so close. He'd gotten her to the Olympic trials. He her mentor, she the eager young rider who rocketed in an amazing rise. Only to have a falling out, have one of her rides end in disaster, the horse injured, rider error blamed though according to the newspaper article Melina had claimed her gelding had been misbehaving all that day.

Misbehaving as Violet's horse misbehaved the afternoon we'd met. To which Melina reacted very, very badly. Because she knew, didn't she? What her former teacher had done, interfering with her student's big, white horse as he'd taught her to do.

I slammed the back door shut, scowling at the ground. I was wrong. I was sure Alphonse was the killer, that he'd taught his protégé what he knew. But without evidence, was I incorrect? Was the gelding really just a bad boy?

No, I found it too hard to accept, especially considering her reaction in hindsight. She'd been furious with Alphonse, not Violet. If the girl had been the cause of the horse's bad behavior, it would have been the other way around.

Did that mean he was the reason Melina's own horse faltered and lost her that run she made for the Olympics? Why sabotage his own rider? Whatever the case, she'd been close enough to SuSu's stall I made a correlation between Violet's Jagger and

Sarah's big mare. It made far too much sense to me Melina chose retaliation against Alphonse through the best route she knew how—the most poetic justice of all.

He must have caught her at it. Challenged her. And she came after him with a loaded syringe, only to have him turn it on her. Who knew? Except, apparently, this entire scenario, as obvious as it was to me, was fallacy at this point. Made up in my head, and more likely that, according to evidence and her already partially admitted guilt, Gretchen did it after all.

I locked his room behind me, the master keys we'd used to do our searches heavy in my hands, and I returned the keys to his car back into the pocket I'd nicked them from, slipping out of his room again before he could catch me. No need for Alphonse to think I'd suspected him, after all, my imagined scenario tucked safely away in the back of my mind where it could only do me harm with occasional jabs as a reminder to pay attention to something I couldn't prove.

Nor could I bring myself to go home, though, returning to the crime scene. The stable had been reopened, a few of the stalls closed over, horses drowsing or munching on hay, the occasional knicker welcoming me as I paced down the walkway to the stall where I'd hidden out, where I'd listened to Robert talk to the woman I believed was Marie Patterson and had a thought.

I glanced in SuSu's stall, noted she'd been ridden

recently, was curious about me but didn't bother coming to the door to greet me. She was a Patterson horse, wasn't she? Sarah said she didn't own her, that she was on loan. So, what if it had been a Patterson who killed Melina? If they discovered her injecting the mare…?

Then again, what if this was entirely unconnected to the doping? That would have been nice, right? I fantasized again, suddenly excited over the possibility of pinning it on the family, of finally having what I needed to get permission to dig into them. Delicious, that thought, though it also prompted worry about Pamela all over again.

Sarah was looking for her aunt. Did that mean the threat Robert alluded to, that the newspaperwoman herself suggested, might have been carried out in some nefarious way to punish her for speaking to me?

Time to focus on what really mattered and let Jill and Liz wrap this case up. I had friends to free from the evil spider's web of the matriarch of the Patterson family.

I didn't register the stirring of the horses, the displacement of air as the door opened, only noting it in the back of my mind as I stood there and contemplated my next moves. It wasn't until a heavy footstep sounded behind me, the wash of heated breath on my cheek making me flinch that I realized something was wrong. I felt myself propelled forward, a wide hand between my shoulder blades shoving me hard into the stall door in front of me, a door that bounced open, jerked wide by my assailant who then pushed me again, this time face-first into the space beyond.

The last time I'd been in this stall it was empty but for the straw on the floor and the body of Melina Canty. This time? This time the towering, and suddenly terrified, form of a giant horse who'd been there first, thank you very much, and wasn't expecting a visitor, loomed over me. I heard the door slam shut in my wake, felt the sting of something against my cheek and watched the vast animal react to whatever it was skimmed by me.

Something shiny and silver and sharp that impacted the shoulder of the large, already unhappy equine. The gelding snorted and squealed before rearing up in front of me, front hooves thrashing, giant head shaking from side to side, teeth bared in rage.

I fell back against the closed stall door, a scream torn from me, arms over my head in a feeble attempt to save me from what would surely be a bloody and painful death at the thrashing, shining shoes of the big horse whose home I'd invaded against my will.

Except, as I lunged to huddle in the corner and make myself as small a target as possible, I heard the sound of running feet, felt the whoosh of air when the stall door swung open and looked up when Sarah, her face tight with worry but her entire body calm and steady, soothed the gelding until he settled.

Still snorting, he backed away from me, a faint line of blood trickling down his neck. Sarah removed the syringe from his skin, turning to stare down at me in shock.

"Fee, what happened?"

I lurched to my feet, the gelding now wavering, clearly in receipt of a dose of what had to be ketamine in that needle. I spun and ran out of the stall, no idea where he'd gone but again certain I had the right attacker, the murderer. And that syringe was my proof.

"Hang onto that!" I exited the barn at a run, heading for the SUV I'd searched, knowing now I'd missed something. Of course, he was old school. I'd been looking for new-fangled. Alphonse probably had a cooler or something unplugged where he kept his supplies.

The same supplies he shared with Melina.

I watched him drive off, ran for the only vehicle I had access to, thankful I still had the keys to Gretchen's big SUV in my possession. The engine fired up and I pursued the coach, not sure where he thought he could escape to and if I'm honest about it, too full of adrenaline to think about what I was doing.

Because chasing him down? About as dumb an act as him trying to run.

I caught up with him, maybe because I was used to the roads and he wasn't, or because I'd chosen to be more reckless. Regardless of the reason, the moment I reached him, barreling down the road in pursuit, I realized I made a huge error.

Sure, I'd caught up with him. But now what?

The answer came in the form of a sign, one I chose to believe was from fate, though it was actually only from the department of transportation. Knowing I only had one shot at it and that if I failed, I could easily kill both of us and, if oncoming traffic didn't get out of the way, someone else, I waited with bated breath until the second sign appeared at my bumper before swinging to his inside, just past his rear end, before jerking on the wheel, hard.

The front end of my SUV took his bumper square and, amid a horrible crash that shook me to the bone, swerved his vehicle to the right and up the runaway ramp created for transport trucks that lost control on the mountain. My plan to simply drive him up the ramp and stop him was overshot when he clearly lost control, swerving and impacting a tree at enough speed it tore the poor evergreen up at the roots, decimating the front of the truck while the explosion of white through the windows told me the airbags had deployed.

I had just enough time to slam on the brakes, jamming the SUV into park, leaping out without shutting off the engine before the driver's side door of the opposing car lurched open and Alphonse Brunbaugh fell out.

CHAPTER TWENTY-NINE

You know, I loved being right. My favorite, every single time. Was the sort of thing that always gave me a thrill, a warm and fuzzy feeling that made life worth living, brightened my existence, justified every little bit of busy bodying I'd ever done for the sake of hell, yes, this was why I snooped, don't mind me, right girl coming through.

Except, of course, when I made stupid, stupid judgments and took action on those judgments because I was feeling that said ridiculously overconfident high from being right.

Yup. I was an idiot who, instead of being careful or cautious or considering even for a second the man who tumbled out of the wrecked truck might still be dangerous to my continuing existence, that even the

SUV itself may have had some sort of mechanical malfunction tied to the massive collision with the collapsed tree it took out that could cause risk or bodily harm, instead thought not at all and rushed toward the crushed and steaming wreck and the staggering man with that self-righteous *I WIN* Flemingness erasing all measure of intelligence and self-preservation from my make-up.

You might argue I was worried he might be seriously hurt. Or that I needed to take him into custody. Even that perhaps the steam coming from the front of the broken SUV might be a precursor to fiery mayhem and impending death. Yes, you might argue that, and I could nod and agree, let you think better of me considering I'd just caught a murderer all on my little lonesome (okay, the big, black SUV played a role but whatever). We could part ways with back pats on my end for a job well done while all the excuses in the world created a fantasy around the fact I was, in truth, an utter and complete fool who didn't have the sense her parents gave her when it came to the absolute need I had to be *right*.

But in the quiet depths of my mind? I knew. Confessed my sins and moved ahead anyway with gusto, faintly hysterical excitement and a penchant for adventure that surely would get me killed one day.

I just wanted to prove I was good enough.

Go me.

All went according to plan, at least in the beginning. I made it to Alphonse as he groaned, his collapsed form rolling over, still on the ground as I approached. Problems only arose as, about a step before I reached him, he managed to surge to his feet. Yup, a mere breath before I had the chance to (what, exactly? No cuffs, no gun, no nothing, Fleming) take him into custody (repeating the previous reminder I had nada wasn't going to help, but mentioning it anyway), he regained control of himself, just as I reached his side.

Here's where the truth of my spiral into ridiculousness and pathetic lack of self-awareness really came into play. I still didn't sense anything was amiss as I finished closing the distance and grasped for his arm. That lack of weapon or any device capable of confining my prisoner (could I call him that if I had nothing to imprison him with? Debatable but bear with me) put me at a distinct disadvantage I was only grasping in that particular moment when all the puzzle pieces of where I was, what I was doing and my lack of support, backup and equipment came into sharp focus. Because it honestly took being in that particular situation, in the then and now, for me to note as he turned toward me, towering over me a moment later much as the angry, terrified gelding had, he was much more dangerous than any horse.

And, in his right hand, held at a threatening level that could easily do me damage? A fully loaded syringe, sharp needle point shining in the last of the daylight.

He wasn't in Melina's office looking for a

threatening letter he'd written. He was taking supplies from her stash. And now I was facing off with the result of his theft.

I tried to step back but he reversed the grasp I had on him, even as I released him his larger, stronger hand grasped my wrist and locked on, holding me so tight I felt the bones grind together. He twisted my arm as his lips mimicked the act, no longer the arrogant if unassuming older man I'd spoken to so many times but instead appearing almost wicked in his shift toward fury.

"You killed her." I should have just kept my mouth shut, except surely someone witnessed the accident and would come looking to see if we were okay. Or call emergency. Or something. Anything. I just had to get him talking and I was good at that, wasn't I?

For a moment I feared I'd misjudged all over again because he didn't seem interested in talking, the syringe hovering over my arm while he jerked me closer. I cried out in pain, the pressure enough, I was sure, he'd break something before too long as I eased myself into the motion and tried to relieve some of the pain when he finally hissed in my face.

"It was an accident." His brown eyes flared wide, nostrils, too, tiny drops of spit landing on my cheeks as he shook me, agony from the motion sending electric-like shocks up my arm and making me sob. He didn't even seem to see me, blurting out his confession that I barely caught as I fought against his grasp, feeling compressed by the pain, out of control, unable to free myself despite the panic growing in my chest. "Everything she knew? She learned from me. And she dared use it against my riders." He shook me hard, and I felt something in my arm let go, the release almost enough to drive me into unconsciousness as the kind of pain I'd never felt before gouged a giant hole in reality and drove blackness around the edges of my vision. "She got me fired, lured Gretchen into doping, blackmailed her into replacing me. Imagine." He almost sounded proud. "I taught her too well. I wanted her to stop. She was going to get us both caught. Her arrogance was going to ruin everything." How had he gone so long without anyone discovering what he'd been doing? Because he was careful which, apparently, Melina hadn't been. Was that why they fell out? Didn't matter now. "But she refused, laughed at me. Said she was going to get me banned. I lost my temper." He seemed to realize what he said and what his actions displayed were mirror images because he eased up slightly. I panted into the pain, still weeping openly, just wanting it to go away, to escape him. I didn't care if he went to prison for what he'd done as long as he let me go.

Please, just make it stop.

His eyes narrowed, face settling into calm as he quickly glanced down the road then back to me. I whimpered in his grasp, no longer fighting. It just hurt too much. But when he jerked on my arm, tugging me further into the woods, I screamed as the latest dose of adrenaline hit my system.

He didn't need to confess what he'd done like so many others had to me over the years. Could have, but it was unnecessary under the circumstances. I was about to force him to relive that scenario with me taking Melina's place.

Did that give him pause at all? Didn't seem to. As surely as it had played out in the stable the day Melina Canty died, that natural flood of chemical enhancement killed the pain in my arm, slowed my heart (in my perception, if not in actual fact), and brought me a clarity I'd never known before.

They'd fought over the syringe, he and Melina. She must have known losing control of it meant her life, as I did. Or perhaps she didn't know, assumed her safety, that the man who trained her, taught her everything she knew, would never really harm her. Did death come as a surprise to her, then? I had no illusions, had come across the evidence of that which this man was capable. Any thought he might spare me died as surely as she had under the overdose influence of the drug he now turned on me.

But surely, she'd fought hard, her body tense, her unwillingness to allow him to harm her giving her added strength. As mine did, with Alphonse's superior weight and power pushing inexorably against my waning ability to hold him off. In that next slow, agonizing moment, I watched the remainder of Melina's life unwind in my head as surely as if I were viewing a tragic movie. He'd stabbed her with the shining needle while she gasped, stared with huge eyes, as I stared. His thumb depressed the plunger. Did he know what he'd done? Maybe not with her. Perhaps he'd instantly regretted what he'd done to the woman he'd known for so long. Didn't stop him from leaving her to die while he ran from the stable, dropping the evidence in the manure pile—by accident, I could only guess— before establishing himself an alibi in the only way he knew how. By illegally breaking into her office, giving himself the kind of excuse only a fool would use and making it sound perfectly plausible.

Did he regret killing me, though, knowing now what effect the overdose would have? Because perhaps he didn't realize he'd done her in that day, not until it was over and too late. But he knew with me. And not a shred of guilt passed through those eyes as he fought to end my life as he'd ended hers.

In that slow-motion review of the attack, I watched the real-time syringe move toward me, watched my free hand rise and deflect it. I'd learned from her, you see, from that woman's demise. I would not go the way she had. Instead of trying to force his hand and superior strength away, as he'd expected, I instead guided his hand inward. He'd been braced to block me from knocking his arm aside. Pulling it toward us met zero resistance.

I think that was shock on his face when the needle entered his leg. Pretty sure it was poetic justice, though when I hit his hand and his fingers flexed. I completed the move and pulled the needle free, a stream of ketamine sparkling from the end of the needle as it exited his flesh, the partial dose he'd received a far cry from the fatal one that had taken Melina's life.

Instead, his hand still grasping my arm, the agony of it returning, with that stare locked on me while consciousness left him, Alphonse Brunbaugh dragged me to the ground with him before passing out, hand rigid and unmoving, though it wouldn't have mattered if he'd let me go on his way down or not.

The pain returned like a gunshot and, I'm not ashamed to say, the moment he passed out, so did I.

CHAPTER THIRTY

My arm hurt, but more, my chest ached. Not from the attack, from the accident—though I had lots of bruises from the events of the previous day, no question, and zero answers as to where those ugly black marks on my legs, torso and back came from. Though my encounter with the horse and being pushed into the stall likely accounted for some of the injuries.

No, this aching pain had nothing to do with the radial fracture of my ulna or the deep thrum of wounds that distracted me enough I needed painkillers to dull the edges so I could function. Rather, the embedded agony I suffered came from the dark, silent front door, locked against me, with the "In Hiatus" sign taped haphazardly to the glass.

The *Reading Reader Gazette* was closed, and I couldn't find Pamela Shard anywhere.

I'd gone looking this morning, started making calls. Especially after waking super early with the pain from my injuries refusing to let me sleep any longer. I'd warranted a stay in the hospital again, though only one night, so there was that bonus, though the look Dad gave me when he drove me home to Petunia's spoke volumes. Even more than the words he used when I slowly, painfully climbed out of his truck into Mom's waiting arms, Daisy's concern fluttering around me as she did.

"He told me to keep you safe," my father said, and I knew exactly who that he was, didn't I? Reference obvious. "You're making me look bad, kid."

Sorry, not sorry.

I'd woken in the hospital emergency room with my bone set (thankfully) and cast in place, grateful in my grogginess to discover they didn't need to do surgery, that the break had been clean enough. The pretty pink wrapping they'd put over the ugly cast wouldn't stay that way long, but at least it appeared cheery enough when Mom caught sight of it tucked into the sling the ER doctor insisted I wear home.

Not that I was arguing. I'd saved my fight with her for my insistence I was fine and that I'd only passed out because of the pain of the pressure on the broken bone. She'd relented, I'd won, my favorite. And yet, as Mom and Daisy settled me in my apartment with my wounded wig tucked into the canvas sling and the pain slowly surfaced, I found myself wishing I'd not fought so hard, after all, and that a morphine drip was at my disposal.

Crew didn't call. I was grateful. Not that he wasn't in touch but that, obviously, the people in my life kept from the man I loved the fact I'd been injured at all. Otherwise, I knew he wouldn't have stopped until he got through to me.

And gave me a piece of his mind. That would wait until he got home and saw what my latest adventure awarded me.

Didn't feel like a prize, though, did it?

In the end, despite the whininess I felt, the need to stay put and nurse my poor, broken arm, it was the desperate text from Sarah that got me up, moving and thinking about something other than the fact Jill and Liz successfully arrested Alphonse, now awake and still in the hospital under careful watch to make sure he didn't suffer untoward side effects from the dose of ketamine he'd had. Aside from the memory loss, that was. Couldn't use it to hide the fact he was a murderer, though.

I wondered if, like the horses he dosed, it made him irritable and misbehaving. Snort.

Okay, so my humor remained, just dampened by my concern for Pamela. Because, naturally, that was the source of Sarah's upset.

"I can't reach her," the young woman said in a voice laced with the level of anxiety that gave me palpitations. "Please, Fee, can you help?"

Did she know I'd been injured? Didn't matter

and was the kind of distraction I needed.

My call to Aundrea Wilkins went unanswered, as did my visit to her house. There was no sign of Alicia at White Valley Lodge, despite the fact she was the manager there. I was told she and Jared were on their honeymoon and had a moment of thought as I slipped behind the wheel of my car, grimacing at the pain as I jostled my arm on the way in. What if Pamela and Aundrea went with them? Was that a ridiculous thought? That question lingered as I made my way downtown and parked, got out of my car, to find myself here, in front of the *Gazette's* front door and the empty darkness on the other side.

Sure, the hiatus could have been due to travel. If the two couples went somewhere together, fair enough. They had enough money they could leave for a month if they chose, though it was so out of character, it gave me pause. Would Alicia even consider abandoning the lodge to her staff for that long? She was a detail freak, like me, had to have things a certain way. Maybe they were just gone a week? After all, the *Gazette* was a weekly paper.

We'd see. Somehow, the silence of the interior, the lack of lights, the hasty sign, made me think something a bit more permanent had happened. Though I hated to think it. Because if some tragedy had befallen Pamela, it was on me. Sure, she'd come to Petunia's of her own accord. But I'd been pushing all along. She'd been warned off, they all had. So, choosing to ask for my help?

Rebellion. And I couldn't help but imagine Marie

Patterson wasn't the sort that took such disobedience lightly.

I dialed Sarah as I turned back to my car. She answered almost instantly, and I hated that I had nothing to tell her.

She sighed when I informed her I'd had no more luck than she had. "I'm off to Florida in the morning," she said. "I've been offered a place to finish my training before the trials." That much was good news. "Can you please keep me posted? I need to know what happened."

I assured her I would, hung up, dejected and in pain, feeling worn out as I leaned against the driver's door of my car and let myself sag a moment. I'd already spoken to Liz and Jill about Pamela, so there wasn't much more I could do. I still had my badge, but I held few illusions about my continuing role as a deputy in Reading. As soon as Crew got back and saw what happened to me, he'd be taking what little authority he'd given me back.

Of that, I had zero doubt.

I climbed back into my car, leaning my forehead on the steering wheel, drawing slow, deep breaths to gain control over the waves of pain I struggled against. Time to go home and take a nice big dose of painkillers, curl up on the sofa and watch TV.

As I sat up, left arm tucked against me, turning the key, I noted the young man approaching with an armload of signs, one of which he proceeded to tape to the front window of the *Gazette's* storefront.

Vivian's faintly smiling headshot stared back

when he was done. *French for Mayor! Vote this November* glared at me from above and beneath the beautiful blonde's image. I drove away, pulling up to the stop sign outside French's Handmade Bakery, mind on the Queen of Wheat, more so when Emile Reis drove past in his little sports car. Maybe I should have had a heavy heart for Vivian and the man who was so in love with her despite the fact she refused to love him back. Instead, I shook my head and pulled through the stop, frustrated enough to flip her establishment my middle finger on the way by.

You know what? She had more than enough going for her and still wasn't happy. She wanted Reading? She could have this town. I was done.

At least Gretchen Latrell was off to jail. Liz happily arrested her, the FBI making her case federal, something that had given the agent a great deal of joy. From what I knew, Charlie was off to his next assignment, though he'd told Liz he was still hunting the source of the stolen ketamine. Alphonse didn't have any of his own, the dose that killed Melina and drugged the older coach had been the victim's purchase and her supplier vanished with her death.

Not my problem and I wished him luck.

I did feel bad for Jimmy/Edward, knew he was now done for life, out of the saddle, out of competition. But I honestly couldn't muster enough empathy to make a difference.

As I parked and exited the car, climbing the steps to Petunia's, I thought about Violet and found myself feeling rather cynical about the fact the arrogant little snot would likely succeed. The one person I openly disliked from the get-go was the only really innocent one if you didn't count Sarah. But even she'd been deceiving the people around her, spying for the committee.

Tangled webs. Made me think of Marie Patterson. Just increased my grump factor.

You know what else made me damned grumpy? Certain people poking their noses into my life. And one of them was sneaking through my foyer when I got home.

CHAPTER THIRTY-ONE

I suppose I should have been grateful to Rose. After all, the sight of her slipping through the kitchen door was a brilliant distraction from the pain of my arm and various bruises. I hurried after her, a head of steam building, Mom's absence from the kitchen clearly the only reason Rose made it through to the backyard without being challenged. I followed, keeping my distance, if only because the feminine half of Rosebert seemed intent on something I now wanted to discover for myself.

She rushed over the bridge, ignoring Fat Benny and his koi buddies, shoes silent on the wood slats, looking right and left as she went but apparently not knowing I was behind her. I kept pace, wincing as I tripped on a flagstone and catching myself and my breath at the edge of the bridge before carrying on.

When I finally approached it was because she'd paused near the back door to the annex, head cocked to one side, clearly listening in to something. I peeked around her, through the screen, expecting Rose was eavesdropping on Mom and Daisy, but what could she possibly want to overhear between those two that put her at risk of discovery on my property?

Instead of Mom's red head, however, the tall, blond man standing so close to Daisy made my breath catch and I realized, in a rush of emotion that brought tears to my eyes, Emile Reis hadn't been talking about Vivian French, had he?

Not when the gorgeous woman I adored looked up at him with that much of her own overwhelming emotion it was obvious she did feel about him the way he felt about her but just couldn't bring herself to do anything about it.

There are times when words aren't necessary, when pictures paint the entire story themselves and in that instant of understanding, as I watched Daisy look down, Emile hand her a single flower that matched her name, then turn with his shoulders slumped, I felt the most powerful heartache of my entire life. Bigger than when Ryan Richards cheated, and I caught him. Bigger than the death of Grandmother Iris. More powerful than anything I'd ever experienced before. Was it the painkillers? My frequent encounters with near-death? Or just the utter truth of how freaking sad the situation actually was that made me want to sob and beg Daisy to tell the handsome guy she'd clearly rejected yet again that she was, in fact, in love with him?

Again, thank goodness for Rose, to be honest, though I wasn't grateful in the moment. She turned as Emile left Daisy with her flowery prize, her nasty face twisted into a smile of bitter satisfaction. And I knew then, again instantly, what role my bestie's evil half-sister played in this whole tragic tale of loneliness and time lost.

She spotted me at the same instant I understood everything. And flinched. Real fear. What look crossed my face? What furious and deathly expression did she see as we faced off over the wretched disservice she'd done to the lovely woman she was supposed to call family, sister? I don't remember what I was thinking, to be honest. No clue if I planned to murder the traitorous little snot or just kick her so hard, she never got back the use of her legs.

Something, surely. Enough to make Rose back off, hands up in front of her as if to ward away impending doom.

"If you set one foot near Daisy ever again," I said, voice low, deep, vibrating, almost unrecognizable, even to me, "I swear, Rose. I swear to you on everything I love and hold dear, I will end you."

She didn't argue, comment, snap back a sullen reply. She just ran.

And I let her go. Because I had to talk to Daisy.

She looked up when I entered the annex kitchen, startled by my appearance. She'd been staring at the heart of the flower she was named for, but now tucked it behind her, hiding it in the folds of her full skirt as she offered one of her trademark smiles that was all my amazing Day.

"Fee!" She came to me, hugging me gently with one arm, careful of my cast, guiding me to sit on a stool. "You should be in bed, silly. Let me get you tea or something." She bustled toward the pot, setting the flower aside, but I interrupted before she could turn on the tap to fill the fat little vessel.

"Day," I said, choked on her name. She looked up, hesitant. Did she know I'd seen? She fluttered a smile, the hiss of water running into the teapot loud enough to mask the shaking in her voice as she spoke.

Or would have to anyone who didn't know her as well as I did.

"We'll just get you situated," she said, all brusque hurrying and kindness, classic Daisy. "Then tucked into bed, okay? I can come watch some TV with you tonight if you want company. You must be missing Crew so much." The teacups rattled as she fumbled with the little metal holders she used for the leaves, her face falling an instant. Was she thinking about love?

Had she been thinking about love all along?

"Day," I said again. "Tell me. Tell me why."

She did know, understood I had seen them together. Stopped what she was doing. Picked up the flower and held it out to me, tears on her cheeks.

"He's not for the likes of me," she whispered. And burst into tears.

Right then and there, I promised myself, no matter what happened, no matter how much it took, Rose would pay. Right after I did everything in my power to erase the damage she'd done by preventing Daisy from finding her happily ever after.

I had zero doubt that's what Rose had been up to, the purpose of the horrible woman's insidious attention since I'd met her. Since she'd known Daisy, obviously. I already was aware that Rose spent their lives together undermining my bestie's ability to believe in herself. I'd done what I could to encourage Daisy to trust her instincts, and it had worked, to a point. Then Rose had to come back into her life, hadn't she? Seeing Daisy's broken heart, feeling her desperate hope crushed and her doubt about her own worthiness winning the battle she should easily have won, I hardened the edges of a new weapon, one I hadn't honed just yet but would find a way to bring to bear. And not just on Rose. Robert, too. They would pay for what they'd done to my Daisy.

We didn't get to talk about it. The door swung open, and Liz hurried in, clearly excited by something. Daisy ducked out, hiding her tears, the agent too wrapped up in her own story to notice. I let my bestie go, but this time it wouldn't be for long. I'd be hunting her down shortly, oh, yes, indeedy-doodle, and we'd be having a long talk about Emile Reis and love.

More so, I'd be talking, and Daisy would be damned well listening.

Liz hesitated as she sat down next to me, well-trained and experienced enough to know she'd interrupted something important. I waved off her soft frown that replaced the delight she'd worn, and she accepted that without question.

I really, really liked Liz.

She helped me across the yard to Petunia's kitchen where we joined Mom and Dad. This time, my father was actually making himself useful, chopping vegetables while Mom rolled out dough for fresh biscuits. I settled on one of the stools while Liz grinned at my father.

"So, I know it's not professional to say it," she said, "but I'm saying it. This was the most fun I've ever had solving a crime." She bobbed a nod. "So there."

Dad winked, pointing the knife at me before resuming his chopping. "Welcome to the cutest town in America," he said, "where murder and mayhem increase tourist traffic."

I wasn't laughing. "Says you."

Dad shrugged but ignored my foul humor. He was focused on Liz. "You give that offer more thought, then, Michaud?"

Right, the job thing. Was she actually considering it, for real?

Apparently, because she hesitated a long moment before resting her chin on her fist and grinning at him. "Give me six months," she said. "Then we'll talk."

What was Dad up to? Why was he trying to recruit Crew and Liz into Fleming Investigations? It was a small company, as far as I knew. And yes, of course, Dad worked outside Reading. Did he have big plans? It wasn't like the caseload at the moment was big enough to keep the three of them busy—or in cash flow—for long.

Or was it? After all, I might have had my name on the letterhead, but I knew little about what my dad actually was into.

Maybe it was time to find out what John Fleming was hiding. Because my dad was always hiding something.

The old fart.

CHAPTER THIRTY-TWO

I tried to do some paperwork, struggling to focus. Too many drugs made me nauseated and foggy while too few had painful consequences and I was still trying to sort out the proper dose. Not to mention trying to figure out how best to maintain things when I did accidentally stumble on the right mix of time and pain pills.

The door to my apartment opened, heavy footfalls thudding toward me. Petunia looked up, whuffing softly under her breath, black triangle ears perked in excitement. She was off the sofa and hustling her fat pug body toward the steps before Crew even came into view. She knew it was him.

Frankly, so did I. But I let her greet him first, watched him crouch to scratch her ruff before he looked up and met my eyes, his blue ones full of love and the last remnants of his sorrow.

That all changed rapidly as he took in my cast, my sling and the dark circles I knew graced the underside of my green eyes. With a soft cry of protest, he hurried to me, kneeling next to the sofa and gathering me with great tenderness and caring into his big, strong arms.

I cried on his shoulder, not meaning to, letting out my frustration at the pain, at missing him and my inability, up to now, to track down Daisy and beat sense into her. She'd vanished on me, hadn't reappeared in two whole days, and I worried avoiding me meant she planned to do something drastic to drive Emile away for good.

Seeing my own love, hugging him at last, being able to breathe him in and feel his heartbeat against my chest, almost made my bestie's issue worse. How much had it broken her to see Crew and me so happy?

Not my fault, but I still felt like a bad friend.

I reluctantly told him everything as he joined me on the couch, Petunia in his lap, his arm around my right side so he didn't risk jostling my cast. Crew listened as Crew usually did, with silence and nods and the occasional stroke of my cheek, lips pressing to my temple, hug tightening in all the right places in the story—were there ever wrong places for a Crew hug? Nope, there weren't—until I wound down—just like I always did—and let him speak.

Only, instead of commenting on my arm, the

case, me putting myself at risk again, even Daisy's predicament, he cleared his throat, voice thick as he spoke.

"I want to tell you why I went to California."

I leaned back and looked up at him, nodding, feeling his sadness, still there, still lurking under the surface of his Crewness.

He looked down at Petunia who gazed up at him with adoration and unselfconscious sweetness while he stroked her little ears, and she groaned her delight at his touch. Jealous of my dog, who, me?

"Michelle's mom." He swallowed. "She was like a mother to me, Fee." Was. Oh, Crew. "She was sick, I had no idea. Just found out."

Again with the *was*. "Crew, I'm so sorry."

He nodded then, digging harder at Petunia's ear while she leaned into him with her eyes closing over in utter bliss. As if devoting his attention to her happiness could lift the grief around him.

"She was so grateful I came, but mad at me, too." My fiancé was matter of fact, but I knew him better than that, the depth of his hurt. Such a tough guy on the outside, but so caring and kind on the inside. "I couldn't *not* go. We went through what happened to Michelle together. I wouldn't have survived it without Carol. Without the family." His hand stopped, fell to his thigh while my pug perked before pawing at him to resume. "I'm glad I got to be there for her. She asked me about you. Was really happy to know I was happy, Fee." He blinked at me, tears in his eyes. "I showed her your picture. She said she thought you looked kind." Crew coughed softly, voice thick. "She died last night."

I held him as best I could with a broken arm while he cried on my shoulder this time and was grateful I could be there for him like he always was for me.

When he was empty, he sat back, nabbing a tissue and blowing his nose, before resuming his attention to my pug, a fact she delighted in once again.

"What about the funeral?" I'd go with him, of course, I would.

But Crew shook his head, faint smile enough to tell me he was already healing.

"Carol made me promise to come home," he said. "So, I did." He exhaled slowly, quietly, resting his dark head on the back of the sofa. "She always said life was for living. And she was right." His arm tightened around my shoulders, and I did my best not to wince when he found one of my bruises. "I love you, Fiona Fleming. And I'm going to love living my life with you."

I wanted to tell him how much that meant to me, was about to, when the door to my apartment slammed open and another set of footfalls approached at speed. This time it was Dad, though, and instead of sorrow or happiness, he looked upset.

Like, really upset, scared mixed with furious tied to frustration. He caught sight of Crew who half-rose, more than likely his cop instincts triggered by my father's entrance and obvious concern. Dad waved him off, settling a bit but not much, his grim gaze resting on me.

"I just heard," he said. "You're not going to like it."

What else was new? A horrible fear broke inside me, and I caught my breath. "Dad. Pamela?" Why did the image of her being found floating face down in Cutter Lake just jab me like a sharpened stake of guilt?

But my father's frown of denial told me the news he had to share was much closer to home.

"No, sweetheart," he said. "It's Peggy Munroe."

Crew scowled instantly, and I thought about Liz's friend, his worries about the woman's vendetta against me. What, had she hired someone on the outside to off me? That sounded so melodramatic in my head I almost grinned.

But Crew wasn't smiling, and neither was Dad. "What happened?"

Dad's big hands closed into fists, his brow low, and he actually looked dangerous standing there, like he was preparing to tear someone apart.

"There was an incident at the prison," he said. Oh my god, did she die? But why would that upset Dad?

Nope, not dead.

"She escaped this morning," he said, while I stared in stunned disbelieve, once and for all realizing I would never, ever get accustomed to the surprises my life had to offer, "and they haven't been able to find her."

Crew reacted before I had the chance to demand

answers.

"How did she escape?"

Dad paced, hands pushing through his gray hair. "She faked sick," he said. "Snuck out of the infirmary. She's an old woman." He turned toward us again, tossed his hands. "They screwed up, underestimated her. And she slipped away from them."

"She must have had help." Crew waited to see if Dad agreed, and my father nodded.

"They're looking into it," he said. "But no one has any answers yet." He glanced at me, tense, uptight. "When they searched her cell for clues as to who might have sprung her, they found some things." He stopped dead, lips tight.

Thanks to Liz I had an idea of what those things might be. "Threats against me."

Crew glanced at me, faintly guilty. "You talked to Liz?"

"Someone thought it was a good idea to fill me in." I patted his hand softly to ease the harshness of those words. "I know why you didn't tell me. But Crew, you need to stop trying to protect me. We both know I'm perfectly capable of getting myself into trouble and hiding things from me only makes it worse."

He nodded then, sighed. "I was going to. Then I got the call from Cali…" He looked up at Dad. "We're going to have to figure out security measures."

My father seemed to agree, but I felt myself relax

for the first time since Liz told me about the old woman's threats, not even realizing until that moment I'd been holding that fear inside me.

"Let her come back to Reading," I said. "We have the advantage. It's a small town, not like she can sneak around. Someone will see her. And we'll be waiting."

Dad and Crew both appeared mollified while I thought about my apartment, about Mila and Pamela and Charlie and how unsecure Petunia's actually was. About the fact I was likely creating false confidence when I knew in my heart if the evil old woman who'd tried to kill me, who'd been a "friend" to my grandmother and Marie Patterson, wanted me dead?

I'd be dead. Bring it.

He slips beneath the water, his hand disappearing while she sobs and screams his name and I hold her and pant for air, the overcast sky cold and uncaring, the dock bobbing beneath me. I look up, see the shadow hovering and for the first time recognize his face the instant before he runs away.

I bolted upright, crying out in pain as I jostled my cast, crying over my arm when I tucked it against my body protectively, though it wasn't the agony of the break that made me weep.

At least I didn't wake Dad, snoring on the couch in the living room. Crew hadn't been able to stay, having to deal with the wrap-up of the investigation, but they both insisted I not be alone. I snuggled my pug for comfort, her moaning concern soft in the darkness, though doing little to ease my pain or troubled mind.

Victor. Vivian. That day at the lake. I'd been trying to figure out who the shadowy figure was, to understand why anyone would run away, would allow Vivian's brother to drown. I'd been triggered so many times the last little while, by men in my life, suspected all along it was a male, though my memories only now, apparently, decided it was time and that I could handle the truth.

I'd been reliving the scene more frequently the past few days, triggered by fear. But I realized now it had less to do with that most terrible of emotions, and more to do with the presence of a taller, stronger male, one who I'd already tied to the dark moment without realizing I'd done it.

That the shadow that let Victor drown that day?

It was Robert.

Which suddenly made his conversation with Marie Patterson come into sharp and clear focus. She'd mentioned something that now made sense in context. How certain facts needed to remain among *just us*. Facts like letting someone die? It explained why she owned him, heart and soul. She knew what

Robert had done. Had been using the knowledge against him, likely his entire life.

I thought about Robert's internal darkness, the hideous black I'd seen within him, the breakpoint line he walked, and how any day now he could literally snap. Was this the cause? Was living with the death of Victor French the reason my cousin was so very broken?

He hadn't killed him, as far as I knew. Dr. Aberstock mentioned a bee sting, an allergy. So, there was that, at least (maybe, possibly, not holding my breath while giving a tiny shred of the benefit of the doubt because I couldn't bring myself to believe Robert capable of murder, not just yet). But why had he let Victor drown in the first place? And what had knowing he'd (okay, fine, call a spade a spade) murdered (or what amounted to it) Vivian's brother that horrible day done to his soul?

Well, I was kind of privy to the state of his soul, wasn't I? Yes, the darkness inside him had to be fed by the guilt of Victor's death. And yet, I had no idea if it was simply cowardice that led Robert to run away or was there a more despicable and undisclosed reason for the boy's demise? One thing was certain. A reckoning was coming. And I'd be delivering the sentence.

With agony making my arm throb, darker thoughts than I'd ever endured keeping me awake, it was a long and lonely night of vengeance planned before I fell back into a fitful slumber filled with the sound of Vivian screaming her brother's name.

The Reading
Reader Gazette

VOLUME 1   ISSUE 1   WWW.RRGAZETTE.COM

ON HIATUS

Looking for more Fiona Fleming? Book twelve, **Something Borrowed, Something Blue and Murder**, is available now!

AUTHOR NOTES

My very dear reader:

As I sign off on the publication of book eleven, I'm anticipating the next six weeks and the wrap up of the **Fiona Fleming Cozy Mysteries**. Thirteen books, thirteen murders, and a giant list of secrets still to uncover.

I literally have goosebumps right now, thinking about all the threads Fee is having me tie together. Book twelve, ***Something Borrowed, Something Blue and Murder*** is going to rock your world. It's already rocking mine. As for book thirteen, well…

So much awesome awaits.

I've had a grand old time with Fee. She's led me on the kind of adventure I wasn't expecting when I first heard her whisper. I wasn't even sure if mysteries were my thing. Sure, that one Nancy Drew novel I'd read back when I was twelve was the very book to wake me up to wanting to be a writer in the first place. And yet, writing cozies is such an art, one I respect immensely.

I've done my very best to honor Fee, her voice and style, and the way she's told me how each tale unfolded. While shivering, laughing, crying and bouncing in excitement over every revelation.

I know you're sad we're almost done. But, I can tell you, while this particular series is finished, I promise this isn't the end of Fiona Fleming. In fact, while I spend the rest of my winter in the south, hiding out on a beach or in a hammock while writing and creating and being happy, it will be with Fee in my head (along with Syd, for you Hayle coven fans) and a few other choice voices who really, really want me to get to it already.

Yes, Fee has another series. You've read hints about it in this volume, in previous ones. With more, as always, to come.

Best,
Patti

ABOUT THE AUTHOR

EVERYTHING YOU NEED TO know about me is in this one statement: I've wanted to be a writer since I was a little girl, and now I'm doing it. How cool is that, being able to follow your dream and make it reality? I've tried everything from university to college, graduating the second with a journalism diploma (I sucked at telling real stories), am an enthusiastic member of an all-girl improv troupe (if you've never tried it, I highly recommend making things up as you go along as often as possible) and I get to teach and perform with an amazing group of women I adore. I've even been in a Celtic girl band (some of our stuff is on YouTube!) and was an independent film maker (go check out the Lovely Witches Club at www.lovelywitchesclub.com). My life has been one creative thing after another—all leading me here, to writing books for a living.

Now with multiple series in happy publication, I live on beautiful and magical Prince Edward Island (I know you've heard of Anne of Green Gables) with my multitude of pets.

I love-love-love hearing from you! You can reach me (and I promise I'll message back) at patti@pattilarsen.com. And if you're eager for your next dose of Patti Larsen books (usually about one release a month) come join my mailing list! All the best up and coming, giveaways, contests and, of course, my observations on the world (aren't you just dying to know what I think about everything?) all in one place: http://bit.ly/PattiLarsenEmail.

Last—but not least!—I hope you enjoyed what you read! Your happiness is my happiness. And I'd love to hear just what you thought. A review where you found this book would mean the world to me— reviews feed writers more than you will ever know. So, loved it (or not so much), your honest review would make my day. Thank you!

Made in United States
North Haven, CT
29 August 2024

56708157R00146